Michael Underwood and The Murder Room

>>> This title is part of The Murder Room, our series dedicated to making available out-of-print or hard-to-find titles by classic crime writers.

Crime fiction has always held up a mirror to society. The Victorians were fascinated by sensational murder and the emerging science of detection; now we are obsessed with the forensic detail of violent death. And no other genre has so captivated and enthralled readers.

Vast troves of classic crime writing have for a long time been unavailable to all but the most dedicated frequenters of second-hand bookshops. The advent of digital publishing means that we are now able to bring you the backlists of a huge range of titles by classic and contemporary crime writers, some of which have been out of print for decades.

From the genteel amateur private eyes of the Golden Age and the femmes fatales of pulp fiction, to the morally ambiguous hard-boiled detectives of mid twentieth-century America and their descendants who walk our twenty-first century streets, The Murder Room has it all. **>>>**

The Murder Room
Where Criminal Minds Meet

themurderroom.com

Michael Underwood (1916–1992)

Michael Underwood (the pseudonym of John Michael Evelyn) was born in Worthing, Sussex and educated at Christ Church College, Oxford. He was called to the Bar in 1939 and served in the British army during World War Two. He returned to work in the Department of Public Prosecutions until his retirement in 1976, and wrote almost 50 crime novels informed by his career in the law. His five series characters include Sergeant Nick Atwell and lawyer Rosa Epton, of whom is was said by the *Washington Post* that she 'outdoes Perry Mason'.

Murder Made Absolute

Michael Underwood

An Orion book

Copyright © Isobel Mackenzie 1955

The right of Michael Underwood to be identified as the author of this
work has been asserted in accordance with the Copyright, Designs and
Patents Act 1988.

This edition published by
The Orion Publishing Group Ltd
Orion House
5 Upper St Martin's Lane
London WC2H 9EA

An Hachette UK company
A CIP catalogue record for this book is available from the British Library

ISBN 978 1 4719 0766 1

www.orionbooks.co.uk

To Anne

CHAPTER ONE

'I THINK that will be a convenient point to adjourn', said Mr. Justice Riley in a tone which brooked no response other than an ill-piped and sycophantic chorus of 'If your Lordship pleases'.

Most judges would have made at least a pretence at consulting the convenience of counsel, but not so Riley, J. With slow deliberation he closed his note-book and then, as if it were an operation requiring the utmost precision, he removed his spectacles and put them into their case with apparent loving care. All the while counsel stood and waited for his detested lordship's exit from the court. The usher had drawn back the heavy faded puce curtain which covered the door behind the judge's seat and whose exclusive purpose was to protect those of Her Majesty's judges who had to sit in that architecturally hideous and acoustically abominable court from the dangerous draughts which seemed to dominate their lives. Despite the curtain, several of the better-worn judges were wont to bring into court an assortment of rugs, mittens, air-cushions and charcoal foot-warmers to mitigate the rigours of trying endless divorce cases in such uncongenial surroundings.

Mr. Christopher Henham, Q.C., stood waiting with the rest. He went through the somewhat formal motion of tidying his papers, but more for want of something to occupy his hands than for any practical reason. His clerk, Alfred Exley, who was hovering in the wings, would

1

collect them together and take them back to Chambers or hand them to Maureen Fox, the Chambers' shorthand-typist and sole female element, to do so. Maureen usually contrived to be in court at the end of the day's sitting and if given half a chance would sit there by the hour listening to Christopher Henham's flights of advocacy which, in her view, were ideally suited to the inevitably sordid drama of a divorce action. His tall commanding presence and his finely modulated voice were able to transport her into erotic reveries as she lingered in court long after completion of the duty which had taken her there. If only, she so often sighed to herself, if only he didn't have to wear that silly wig in court. It detracted from his exemplary looks and hid his thick smooth thatch of iron-grey hair which was infinitely more impressive than the wig, which now resembled a seedy mop more than a head-dress. And if only he could also get rid of that dreadful cough.

Mr. Justice Riley was at last ready to make perfunctory acknowledgement of counsel's bows. As he did so his eye glinted at the sight of Christopher Henham carefully putting his cough capsules back into their container. He always rolled three or four out on to the desk in front of him so that they were readily available when he felt his maddening and almost permanent throat tickle about to develop. It was the sort of tickle that quickly became a body-convulsing cough with a totally stultifying effect on the minds of all within earshot.

'Er . . . Mr. Henham', purred the judge in his silkiest tone. Christopher Henham looked up, at the same time screwing the cap back on to the tube of capsules and slipping it into his trouser pocket.

'M'Lord?'

'May I suggest that before we resume this case to-morrow, you provide yourself with something rather more efficacious for your troublesome throat.' He spoke in the slow, deliberate tone which so infuriated many of the advocates who appeared before him. Nothing would ever make him hurry it and nothing could alter the course of a sentence once he had embarked upon it. 'Perhaps you could even be persuaded to sample one of my brand of throat pastille. They certainly can't be less effective than your capsules.' Here his wintry smile became even less attractive. 'And I can at all events assure you, Mr. Henham, that *mine* contain no harmful drugs.'

Christopher Henham, who had known Gethin Riley for over a quarter of a century, had shared Chambers with him until his recent elevation to the Bench and still had a neighbouring week-end cottage, knew better than to show any visible sign of annoyance at the judge's chosen pastime of pin-pricking friends, acquaintances and enemies alike. It was as much a part of his nature to do so as a cat's to toy with a mouse and had provoked some wit into remarking that even Gethin's best friends couldn't stand him.

'Your Lordship is most kind', he said as the judge turned to go. A moment later he sank back on to his seat and blew out his cheeks in a gesture of exhausted patience. 'He gets more objectionable every day', he said to the barrister next to him. 'I very nearly dropped my brief and walked out of court at one point this afternoon.'

The other nodded thoughtfully. 'Of course you couldn't be on a stickier wicket. He's always very much a petitioner's judge where the petitioner is a woman, and your client didn't make an awfully good showing.'

Christopher Henham grunted. 'Still no reason for him to visit the sins of the respondent on his hapless advocate.'

'Oh, granted he's not a good divorce judge. I some-times wonder if they shouldn't take some sort of course to purge them of their more obtrusive moral principles. Now old Pelsey was a first-class divorce judge and no one

3

can have taken a broader view of life than he. Well I must get back to Chambers. Got a conference. See you tomorrow morning, Henham.'

Christopher Henham lifted his wig by the point of his pencil and scratched his head with his free hand. By now he and Maureen were the only two people left in court.

'We'd also better get back to Chambers, Maureen. I'm afraid I shall have to dictate an opinion this evening and I must have it by first thing tomorrow morning.' He looked up at her. 'O.K.?'

'Yes, that'll be all right, Mr. Henham. I haven't got anything special on tonight so I can easily stay late and do it.'

'That's fine, though I'm terrified that one day I shall have one of your boy-friends after me with a gun for having been the cause of your breaking a date.'

Maureen made no reply to this kite-flying remark but continued to gather up his scattered brief and collect the various legal volumes which had to be taken back to Chambers. Christopher Henham watched her through half-closed eyes. She must have boy-friends, he thought, though she rarely mentioned their presence in her life and then rather by implication than by direct reference. She certainly possessed her fair quota of physical charm but his guess was that she would give short shrift to those who were interested only in that aspect of her endowments. As she leant across to pick up a book from the seat beside him, he held his breath and was conscious only of the enticing fragrance of her presence. She stood back and looked at him.

'Are you coming back now, Mr. Henham?'

'Yes, I'll walk across with you.'

Together they walked down the long, stone corridor, Christopher Henham with the long, easy stride of an athlete and with his body slightly bent forward so that he didn't look his full six feet two inches. Maureen's heels clicked at his side with a quick purposeful rhythm and she seemed to have no difficulty in keeping up with him. She, too, was tall. She had an oval face, a full mouth and wide, clear eyes. Her dark hair was cut short, waved in front and neat-fitting at the back. When they reached the robing-room at the entrance to the Royal Courts of Justice, Christopher Henham said:

'While I'm getting my robes off, you might go across to the chemist's and get me another tube of cough capsules. You know the ones, Capstick's, the three-and-sixpenny size.'

A few minutes later they met outside the shop and as they dived down one of the alleyways leading into the Temple, Maureen handed him the tube of capsules and said:

'You're not going to try something fresh after what the judge said?'

'I am not. Gethin Riley, sitting on the Bench, looking like a squat Buddha and sucking those beastly Umujubes of his—they sound like a Mau Mau blood oath anyway – doesn't know what a persistent cough and throat tickle is. These capsules I take are not just lollipops, they're a proper medicine.'

'Oh', said Maureen. 'I've never understood how something you swallow can help your throat.'

'It's very simple. The capsule melts in the tummy and the' – he was about to say drug when he suddenly recalled the judge's malicious observation on the subject and instead went on – 'contents are released. They become absorbed into the blood stream and so soothe the throat nerves which, in my case, are the niggers in the woodpile, if you'll forgive the startling metaphor.'

'I see', said Maureen, adding with diffidence and lack of logic, 'It's funny the way Mr. Riley has changed since he became a judge. Of course I hardly knew him. I'd only just arrived in Chambers when he was appointed but I would never have thought —'

Christopher Henham didn't wait for her to finish the sentence but broke in: 'Mr. Riley, as you call him, and he'd cheerfully give you five years for that if he'd heard you, hasn't changed one little bit. It's just that his present position provides him with bigger and better opportunities for his favourite pastime of gently baiting his fellow-creatures.'

'Well, I don't think it's a very nice way to behave.'

'You're quite right, my dear, it's not.'

'I'm sure he doesn't treat his wife like that.'

Christopher Henham smiled. 'Don't worry. Helen Riley may be diminutive in size but she's fully capable of looking after herself', he said slowly.

On arrival at Chambers, he went to his room, a large, light one with an oblique view of the river. Almost everything in it was either leather-bound, leather-topped or just plain leather. He tilted back his desk chair and slowly started to dictate into the microphone of the recording-machine, at the same time gently swivelling himself from side to side. The recording-machine was a new toy which, though spurned by some in Chambers, was still one of the joys of Christopher's life. As he now dictated his legal opinion he watched the thin brown disc revolving slowly on the turntable while the recording-arm silently transmitted his words on to it. Later Maureen would trundle the machine away to the clerks' room and by the mere turn of a switch reverse the process so that the record played back through the microphone the words he was now confiding to it. When he had finished, he touched the bell (leather-encased) on his desk and a moment later Alfred Exley, his senior clerk, came in.

'I've dictated that opinion for Lawford, Alfred, and

Maureen has promised to stay late and do it, as they must have it tomorrow. She's not only a good girl but also a delightful acquisition to Chambers, eh Alfred?'

The clerk gave his senior member of Chambers a look of faint disapproval but refrained from comment, and Christopher Henham, who knew that he still regarded the presence of females in Chambers as a dangerous innovation, went on, 'Let's see, what's the time now?' He looked at the travelling-clock on the mantelpiece, snug and warm in its leather case. 'Twenty to six. Well, I'm off in a minute or so, Alfred. Anything else?'

'No, sir.' He paused and then said, 'I'm sorry Sir Gethin gave you such a rough ride in court to-day. One doesn't like to see that sort of thing coming from an old member of these Chambers.'

'Probably indigestion', said Christopher Henham lightly. Alfred Exley shook his head sadly and departed. When he had gone, Christopher Henham walked over to the mantelpiece and gazed thoughtfully at the photographs of two women, one at each end. On the left was the first Mrs. Henham and on the right was the present one. It had struck many as a little odd, if not downright tasteless, that he should display photographs of both his wives. But Celia, bless her, certainly didn't mind; and it wasn't as if he'd left Zena to marry Celia. Zena had died and then he had married Celia – four months later. Unhappily tongues are always ready to wag and there had been a good deal of malicious gossip about the fortuitous timing of Zena's death. There was a knock on the door and Maureen came in.

'Mr. Exley says you've dictated that opinion, Mr. Henham. I can get on with typing it straight away.'

'Well done. Here it is.' He handed her a brown, wafer-thin record and gave her hand a fleeting caress with his own as he did so.

7

'Isn't it Mr. Lawford's cocktail-party tonight?' she asked eyeing the invitation on the mantelpiece.

'Yes and I don't much want to go.'

'But won't Godfrey Luce be there?'

'That's the reason I'm not keen on going.'

Maureen looked surprised and clearly regarded his lack of enthusiasm for meeting so renowned an actor as Godfrey Luce as something approaching *lèse-majesté*. He continued, 'It's not a good thing to meet one's lay clients socially before trial, and after trial — Well, after trial they're either so overcome with pleasure at the result that they allow themselves to be borne away by an army of congratulating friends never to be seen again, or else they go off utterly depressed and discouraged by defeat, unshakably determined never to set eyes again on their unsuccessful advocate. In the latter case they sometimes manage to derive slight comfort from the knowledge that they never thought very highly of his ability in the first place.' Maureen gave him an amused but disbelieving smile and he went on, 'The divorce action of Luce, husband, against Luce, wife, is going to be a full-scale Roman circus when it starts and until then, if not for all time, my interest in it is purely professional.'

'But you must go to Mr. Lawford's party. I know I'd love to anyway,' she said wistfully.

'I wish we could go together. As it is I'll probably look in for a short while and slip away as soon as I decently can.'

'But doesn't your wife object if you do that?' Maureen asked with more curiosity than tact.

'Oh, Celia will be all right. She knows the position and has arranged for her ex-husband to escort her. He very conveniently arrived back from East Africa three days ago', he said with a wry smile.

Maureen blushed and felt confused by this bald

8

statement of intimate fact which her question had provoked and Christopher Henham went on, 'And I have no doubt that my stepson will also be there to look after his mother.'

'Yes, he told me he was going.'

'Did he?' It was Christopher Henham's turn to be taken by surprise. 'Robin told you?'

Maureen nodded and managed to make it clear that she was not proposing to elucidate how Robin King-Selman came to inform her of his social engagements.

The telephone rang and he picked up the receiver to hear Alfred Exley's voice speaking from the switchboard in the clerks' office.

'Lady Riley would like to speak to you, sir. Shall I put her through?'

'Yes, do.' He motioned Maureen to leave and she did so. 'Hello, Helen, how are you, my dear?'

In the clerks' office Alfred Exley put down the receiver and switched himself off from their conversation as Maureen came in. He appeared to be lost in deep contemplation and shook his head sadly.

CHAPTER TWO

CELIA HENHAM put down her glass and went to the drawing-room door. Putting her head round the corner, she shouted up the stairs.

'Robin – ROBIN!'

A faint reply floated down from the top of the house and she called out again.

'Do hurry up, darling. It's nearly half past six, and the champagne cocktails will be off if we don't get there soon.' She closed the door and came back into the room. 'And there'll just be one of those insipid lukewarm orange concoctions', she added as she sat down again. 'Dick Lawford always runs his parties on the same orthodox lines as the Biblical marriage feast.'

'You don't look a minute older than – than when I last saw you three years ago', said Marcus King-Selman, studiously ignoring his ex-wife's meanderings.

'How sweet of you to say that, Marcus', she replied, with every appearance of genuine pleasure at the compliment. She gave him a warm, friendly smile. 'Here, let me put the decanter beside you and you can help yourself.' She sat back and gazed appraisingly at her ex-husband. 'And you haven't changed at all either. You're still the healthily tanned, outdoor type who never shows his years.'

'You make me sound like an advertisement for strong tobacco.'

'But, darling, that's just what you do look like and it's madly attractive.'

'That hasn't much ring of truth about it.'

'Oh, Marcus, I mean it. Honestly, I do. Just because —'

'The type is not your cup of tea, you mean?'

'Well, darling, I've always kept hoping that you'd find a nice wife and —'

'I found one once but she tired of the position.'

'Don't put it like that, Marcus. You make it sound so brutal and callous.' Celia frowned at her empty glass. 'You know I never wanted to hurt you. I did everything I could to prevent any bitterness.'

'Yes, I know you did. You effected a very smooth changeover. It's not your nature to hurt anyone deliberately.'

'Thank you, darling.'

'Unless you can't help yourself.'

'Hadn't we better talk about something else?' Celia said. 'We don't want to upset ourselves just before a cocktail-party.'

'Agreed, but just let me say this and then I'll leave the subject. You know that I still love you.'

'Yes, I know you do', said Celia quietly and looked away.

'How's Robin getting on up at Cambridge?' he asked, in an unnaturally brisk tone.

'I think he's working too hard. He doesn't play any games and chemistry is all he seems to think about.'

'He's obviously very delighted with that lab. you've fitted out for him at the top of the house.'

'He spends his whole time up there. Really, Marcus, I think you ought to have a word with him about it. It can't be very healthy. Anyway, it's not natural for a boy of twenty-one to be so single-minded – about something like chemistry, I mean. Apart from which I never feel safe when he's up there.'

'Safe?'

'Every moment I expect this part of Kensington to explode into a large billowing mushroom cloud.'

'I don't think he's doing anything as dangerous as splitting atoms.'

'I only hope that, if he does blow us all up, my radioactive ashes will gently settle on someone really deserving.'

'Such as?'

'Sir Gethin Riley.'

Marcus King-Selman, who didn't know the judge, hadn't sufficient interest to inquire into the whys and wherefores of Celia's dislike of him.

'How does Robin get on with Henham?'

'Do call him Christopher, darling. I can't bear hearing you call him by his plain surname. It sounds so awfully military and masculine.'

'Anyway, how does Robin get on with him?'

'Christopher's awfully good to Robin. No stepfather could have been better in fact; tactful and at the same time interested in him without seeming to interfere.'

'And Robin, what does he think?'

'Robin's going through a difficult phase,' replied Celia after a pause, 'and one has to make allowances. To be absolutely frank, he hasn't made much effort to meet Christopher half-way. Sometimes he seems almost resentful of his presence in the house.'

'Perhaps that's not so surprising. The children are always the chief sufferers in a divorce.'

'But Christopher's been so good to him.'

'Perhaps it might be a good idea if he came out and spent the long vac. with me.'

'But isn't Africa awfully hot in the summer?'

Further discussion about their son was forestalled by his arrival.

'I'm ready, Mummy. Sorry if I've kept you. Good evening, Father.'

''Evening, Robin.'

'Just look at your suit, darling', said Celia, brushing the lapels of his jacket with her hand. 'You look as though you've been rolling in gunpowder.'

'It's only talc de Chanel.'

'That makes all the difference. And, darling, take that horrid thing out of your pocket, it looks too absurd.'

'That's my pipe, Mummy —'

'So it is but you can't possibly smoke it at a cocktail-party. Anyway not until Dick Lawford gives you the signal that he wants his guests fumigated.'

'You used not to wear spectacles, used you?' asked King-Selman, looking at his son.

'He still doesn't all the time', said Celia. 'It depends on his mood.' She turned to Robin. 'Go and bring my car round to the front, darling, while I do a final titivate.'

Robin King-Selman stood pressed into a corner of the room and wished he hadn't come to the party. He was not gregarious by nature and the various conversational gambits required at such functions were alien to him. The two women to his right were obviously bosom friends from their conversation, bits of which drifted across to him, and he envied them the warmth of their friendship. He longed for the comfort of his pipe and kept on nervously fiddling with the forelock of his straight but springy hair which already was showing slight signs of thinning. Suddenly he heard his name being spoken.

'You look as though you dislike these functions, Robin.'

He turned. 'Good evening, Lady Riley. Yes, I'm

afraid I lack most of the social graces necessary for their enjoyment.'

'I see your mother's here.' As she spoke, they both looked across at Celia who was the centre of a small group, and obviously holding the floor and thoroughly enjoying herself.

'She loves parties', Robin said gloomily.

For a time Helen Riley kept up a flow of light inconsequential chatter which he found diverting. He noticed that all the while she was talking, her bright eyes were ceaselessly on the rove. Frequently she shot up on tiptoe to take in an arrival or departure and whenever she did this, she pressed herself very slightly against Robin, and her funny little hat, a sort of sequined skull-cap on the crown of her head, bobbed just below his nose.

'Ah, your stepfather's arrived', she said suddenly, and Robin saw their host immediately rush forward to greet him. A world-famous actor and a fashionable 'silk' were a fine pair of lions to have at a party. Helen Riley drained her glass and held it out to Robin. 'Would you – a dry martini, but not out of that large jug. Tell the barman it's for me and he'll mix it specially.' She bestowed upon him a winning smile to charm him on his way to the bar. When he returned with her drink he found her busily engaged in conversation with a tall lean man who was the shape of a spoon. She took the drink with a brief word of thanks and Robin found himself alone once more.

Twenty minutes later when Celia looked round for her husband, she saw him talking to Helen by the door. A little later he joined her and Marcus King-Selman ostentatiously left her side and walked across the room to where Robin was now exposed to the hearty wiles of a large bouncing girl, his features glazed with an expression of hopeless boredom.

'I'm going, Celia', said her husband in a hissed whisper.

'Have just one more for the road, darling. I've hardly seen you since you arrived. Anyway, where are you going?'

'Probably have dinner at the club and then I've got to go back to Chambers to pick up some papers.' He took a glass of pale brown liquid from a passing tray. 'Hold this a moment', he said, handing it to his wife. Then taking a tube of cough capsules from his pocket, he shook one into the palm of his hand and washed it down with the cocktail. 'About all this concoction is fit for', he said, making a face.

'Did you drop in at the club on your way here?'

'Yes.'

'For fortification?'

He laughed. 'No, for restoration. Gethin was an absolute pig in court to-day and it took several large pink gins to put the world straight again.' He took a quick look round the room to find his host. 'And now I really will be off, otherwise I know I shall get forced into a social huddle with the great Godfrey Luce. 'Bye for the moment, sweetheart. Here comes your ex to look after you again', he whispered as he moved away.

'Bye-bye, darling', said Celia as Marcus arrived once more at her side. 'It's rather like a badly constructed play, isn't it?' she added, turning to him.

'What is?'

'As one character walks off the stage, another enters for no apparent reason.'

'There's every reason in this case.' He paused and then said with dramatic suddenness, 'Are you sure Henham's faithful to you?'

'What an extraordinary question to ask at a cocktail-party, Marcus. You must be a little tight.'

15

'*He* certainly is.'

She looked at her ex-husband in silence for a moment and then said very seriously, 'Now let's get this straight once and for all, darling. I'm terribly fond of you still and I desperately hope it can always be like that, but Christopher is my husband and I love him dearly. There's nothing I wouldn't do for him, nor he for me, I believe.' She stopped and seemed to study the toes of her shoes. When she looked up again her mood was back to normal. 'And now let's have another drink. Oh, Marcus, just look', she suddenly wailed. 'All those clouds of smoke over there. Robin's lit his pipe.'

Maureen Fox pulled the cover over her typewriter and looked at her watch. It was ten past nine. Apart from the occasional melancholy call of a passing tug on the river, the Temple was encased in deep silence. Here and there a lighted window shone forth and marred the natural serenity of a warm April evening, indicating either a late worker or the tranquil pursuit of leisure by one of its denizens.

She picked up the legal opinion which she had just transcribed and decided she had better put it on Christopher Henham's desk as he had said that he might call back for it later that evening. This done, she put on her coat, made sure the office safe was locked and started for the door. In the small lobby she paused and then on the impulse of the moment, turned and re-entered Christopher Henham's room. She stopped just inside the door and stood there hesitant, not daring to turn on the light. Somehow she felt that she was an intruder, a snooper, and she was filled with disgust at the primeval and irresistible impulse which held her there. It was several moments before she could summon up sufficient will to break the spell. As she closed the door behind her, she murmured out loud to herself, 'You'd better watch out, Maureen my girl, you're in danger of putting yourself on the rack.' Deep down within her a small voice responded with a cynical chuckle.

As soon as she reached the pavement and turned toward the Strand, she saw the car. It was the only one in sight and she at once recognized it as Celia Henham's. It was about fifty yards away and parked on its correct side of the road – her side of the road, in fact. For a moment she drew back into the entrance to Chambers and stood there expecting to see Christopher Henham get out and come toward her. But nothing stirred and she began to feel that its sidelights were mocking her with their unblinking, sightless stare. She licked her lips and stepped across the pavement into the road which she crossed diagonally, reaching the opposite pavement only just before she came level with the car. She hoped she had given a nonchalant performance and suddenly she blushed as the thought came to her that she had probably behaved in this studied fashion for nothing, since the car was almost certainly empty. That was it, she decided, he must be visiting someone in one of the flats in the block outside which it was parked. As she passed, she took a quick look and then her heart really did miss a succession of beats for in the front two people were locked in a lover's embrace. She could just discern the top of Christopher Henham's head but all she could see of the woman was the indistinct outline of the back of her head and shoulders. As Maureen went by the woman's head moved slightly and her small spangled cap caught the light and twinkled momentarily.

The shock of the scene sent Maureen's thoughts plunging about her head like frenzied dolphins. By the time, however, that she emerged into Fleet Street the processes of rationalization were beginning to take charge.

She decided that the impact of the scene upon her had been the greater because of the rather peculiar state of mind she had been in on leaving Chambers. After all, she reasoned, there was nothing very sinister in an eminent Q.C. warmly embracing his wife in a car in the Temple; an unusual sight perhaps, but nothing more and certainly not one which a sensible girl like Maureen should allow to upset her.

As she jumped on to her bus, two things happened simultaneously in London five miles apart. In the car, Christopher Henham sat back and slowly wiped lipstick from his face and at Dick Lawford's party Celia Henham held out her glass for another cocktail and hoped that her husband was somewhere enjoying himself as much as she was.

CHAPTER THREE

CELIA shut the garage doors and walked round to the front of the house. She could see from a light at the attic window that Robin was at play in his laboratory and she presumed that her husband had also arrived home. She felt at one with the world and brimming over with warm, friendly feelings toward all mankind. She found slight difficulty in inserting the front-door key into the lock and was undecided whether to giggle or be irked.

She had barely entered the house and locked up when there was a ring followed immediately by a firm knock on the front door. There was nothing particularly menacing about the knock but its quality of firmness quite definitely impinged upon her mind as she went back into the hall. She switched on the porch light and opened the door wide. On the threshold stood two uniformed police officers. Neither looked over thirty and each, she was relieved to observe, had a pleasant, friendly face. She noticed that they wore flat caps and looking past them she saw their patrol car parked at the kerbside.

'Good evening, madam', said the shorter of the two. 'I'm sorry to bother you at this hour but we're inquiring about an accident which took place a short time ago in Gloucester Road.' Celia said nothing but stared at the speaker with polite interest. He continued, 'Are you Mrs. Christopher Henham?' She nodded. 'And are you, madam, the owner of a car whose registered number is ZIZ 919?'

19

Celia gave a small helpless giggle.

'You sound just like a policeman', she said. The two officers exchanged a quick look and when she went on she noticed that the shorter one's expression had perceptibly hardened. 'I'm sorry, I didn't mean to be rude but I've never thought of my car in quite such formal terms before. Won't you come in and sit down?' She looked from one to the other.

'Thank you, madam, but I don't think that will be necessary', said their spokesman in such a tone that Celia wondered exactly what he thought she'd suggested. 'Have you been out in your car this evening, madam?'

'Yes', she said slowly.

'And just got home?' She nodded. 'I wonder if we might have a look at your car, madam?'

'Certainly. I'll get the garage key.'

She accompanied them to the garage and opened the doors. Side by side stood her Rover and her husband's Rolls Bentley, each giving the shining appearance of the showroom. The officers took a passing look at the rear number-plates, then went round to the front of the Rover. The shorter one turned to the other.

'Got your flashlight, Bob?'

To Celia's fascination Bob conjured up an enormous torch from somewhere in the hinterland of his uniform and directed its beam on to the nearside wing of the car where, they could now all see, the beautiful apple-green paint was scarred by an ugly graze.

'Probably caused by the pedal', he said quietly to Bob. Just below the graze was a short black smear which looked as though it might have been caused by friction with some rubber object. After studying the damage with infinite care for a few moments, Bob started to record details of the licence and the shorter one opened the driver's door and got into the car. There was a nasty thud and a strangled oath as his knee and the steering-wheel met each other. This time Celia managed to stifle her giggle, though she longed to tell him what a ridiculous sight he looked.

'I think you'd be more comfortable, officer, with the seat further back. The catch is just there', she said, pointing beneath his tightly flexed right thigh.

'Thank you, madam, but that won't be necessary', he said as he got out with considerable care. He straightened himself and fixing Celia with a mild but concentrated expression, went on, 'Would you care to explain how the wing of your car became damaged?'

She hesitated a moment. 'It's nothing very serious, is it?' she asked. 'The accident, I mean.'

'That's not for me to say, madam.'

'No, I suppose not; but no one's been seriously injured as a result of this?' She pointed vaguely in the direction of the damaged wing.

'I probably oughtn't to say this——'

'I promise I'll treat it as off the record', she broke in quickly.

'He's been taken to hospital but it doesn't seem to be anything very serious – a few bruises and lacerations.'

'Thank heavens', she said with relief. 'And what's the next step?'

'I'll have to report the matter and then it'll be up to my superiors to decide whether or not to institute proceedings.'

'What sort of proceedings?'

'That depends on the evidence, madam; dangerous driving, careless driving, failing to report an accident. Anyway I must formally warn you that consideration will be given to prosecuting you for offences under Sections 11 and 12 of the Road Traffic Act.'

'Must you?'

'It sounds more formidable than it is', he said with a faint smile. 'It's just a routine warning, required by the statute. The idea being that you can start looking for any witnesses who you think can help your case and are not totally unprepared when a summons is served on you in maybe several weeks' time.'

'What on earth's going on down here?'

Celia and the officers turned to find Christopher Henham standing in the garage doorway. He had on his raincoat with the collar turned up to hide the fact he was partially undressed.

'Oh, it's all right, darling', said Celia quickly. 'I had the tiniest little accident on my way home and these officers have just called to see me about it.' Before he could say anything, she went on hurriedly, 'Look, just a very small scratch on the nearside wing.' She turned to the two officers. 'This is my husband. He's a Queen's Counsel.'

'Good evening, sir', they said in respectful unison, their spokesman continuing: 'As your wife has told you, sir, we're making a few inquiries about an accident in which her car was involved earlier this evening. I suppose you weren't with her by any chance?'

He shook his head and Celia said:

'I was driving alone at the time. Now I'm sure the matter can be very safely left in your capable hands, officer, and I suggest we all go in and have a drink.'

'It's very kind of you, madam, but my colleague and I are still on duty and we must get back on patrol.'

At the front of the house, they exchanged goodnights and Christopher and Celia watched them drive away before closing the front door.

'Now, darling, tell me all about it', she said, flinging herself into an arm-chair, kicking off her shoes and wiggling her toes with obvious enjoyment. 'Why did you take my car from Dick Lawford's party? You know how I hate driving that huge thing of yours.'

'I'm terribly sorry, sweetheart, but when I left mine was completely bottled up, and I didn't want to come back into the house and provoke a game of dodgems round the drive. It seemed simplest to take yours, as I knew you'd understand.'

'I guessed it was something like that.'

There was silence for a moment and then Christopher Henham said:

'Well?'

'The police?'

'Yes. Why did you let them think it was you who was driving the Rover this evening? It could turn out to be rather awkward.'

'I don't see why. Only you and I know the truth and I'm quite happy to stand in the dock and be fined forty shillings . . .' She looked at her husband with wifely tenderness. 'From the very outset they seemed to assume I was the driver: I suppose because it was my car which was involved and – well, I didn't want to bring you into it without knowing exactly what had happened. I pumped them as discreetly as I could.'

'But such altruism?'

She looked at him in surprise.

'Darling, you are being obtuse. Surely I'm much better able to stand this rap than you are. In the first place there'd be all the publicity. "Famous Q.C. on car charge" and worse. And secondly I can't believe it would do your practice or judicial prospects very much good to get involved in a criminal case, albeit a minor motoring one. After all, darling, I know much more about magistrates' courts than you do. Hardly a quarter goes by without my being summoned for parking in the wrong

23

place and that sweet old magistrate at West Central simply adores my visits. We always have such a cosy time together. Besides which, I couldn't bear to think of you in the dock of a police court; you'd be like Gulliver pegged down by the Lilliputians, struggling, quite at sea and rather pitiful.'

There followed a silence in which Christopher Henham gazed thoughtfully at the carpet. At last he said quietly:

'You're a wonderful wife and a very sweet person. Thank you. Thank you very much for what you've done. You deserve to be ranked with Joan of Arc.'

Celia beamed happily and came across and kissed him. Suddenly she started back.

'Your hand, darling? What have you done to it?'

He held out his left hand and studied his thumb which was heavily strapped in plaster.

'Oh, it's nothing much – just sprained my thumb. I slipped on the kerb as I was getting out of the car and tried to do a sort of pirouette on it.'

'Who strapped it up?'

'I went into an all-night chemist's and the chap there did it. I'll go and see the doctor if it gives any bother.'

'You poor darling, what a beastly day you've had. Let's go to bed and you must tell me just how horrid Gethin Riley was to you.' They got up and he started switching out the lights.

'In effect he accused me of being a drug addict.'

'In court?'

'Yes.'

'Isn't that libel or do I mean slander? Anyway, can't you sue him or get the Lord Chancellor to remove him?'

'I fear that neither course is very practicable.'

24

'Are he and Helen going down to their cottage this week-end?'

'I believe so.'

'What a bore. I do wish they weren't our neighbours down there.'

'They're almost more than that. We share a gardener and have no dividing fence between our properties.'

'Let's build a super Maginot Line and shut them out.'

He laughed. 'I've known Gethin for long enough to know how to cope with him without such extreme measures.'

'I still think it was a scandal that he was made a judge before you.'

'Don't let's start that one all over again.'

'But to call you a drug addict in public, darling.'

'He didn't say so in that many words. He just made some disparaging remarks about the effectiveness of my cough capsules and gave his own jujubes a little puff by saying that they didn't contain any harmful drugs. The clear implication being that mine did!'

'Incidentally I bought you another tube of them this afternoon, darling.'

'I got one as well, so I'm well stocked for the next few days.'

Slowly they mounted the stairs together, each with an arm round the other's waist.

'And how is my predecessor?' he asked, as they reached the half-landing.

'Very fit and immensely strong.'

They both laughed.

'You really are a very remarkable woman.'

'I'm so glad.'

'Not many could manage a husband and an ex-husband the way you do without early bloodshed on the part of one of the trio.'

25

'That's because we all trust each other.'

He looked at her in mock astonishment. 'That remark is either extremely naïve or super-cynical.'

'Time will show which', said Celia gaily as she closed their bedroom door behind them.

CHAPTER FOUR

IT was one glorious summer's afternoon in 1937 when Gethin Riley first drew Christopher Henham's attention to the advertisement in *The Times*. At the time each was a highly successful junior member of the Bar with a large, lucrative practice. Often they had discussed together the need for country cottages to which they could retreat at week-ends for recuperation in the soothing atmosphere of the English countryside. The advertisement in question stated that there was just under an acre of land for sale and, in effect, that it was ideally suited to the erection of a country home for a tired captain of industry. On that particular hot afternoon it succeeded in conjuring up in the mind's eye of each a veritable oasis of Elysian fields and they immediately agreed that no time should be lost in further investigation.

Twenty-four hours later Helen Riley had visited the scene and returned enthusiastic about its situation. It was near the river and yet above flood-level and just what they'd been dreaming of for the past two years. No sooner had they bought the piece of land than they agreed the exact sites for their respective cottages, and after some further discussion decided that they would treat the garden as one and not spoil its homogeneity by an artificial dividing line.

They had two glorious summers there during which they frequently blessed the day that Gethin Riley had spotted the advertisement. Then came the war and the two wives (Zena Henham was alive at that time) spent months on end down there, busying themselves in local village life and descended upon at odd intervals by their respective husbands, who were assisting the war effort in differing capacities. Christopher Henham was a lieutenant-colonel in the Judge-Advocate-General's Branch and Gethin Riley a high temporary civil servant in the Home Office.

After the end of the war they were seen at the cottages only at infrequent intervals, but with the derationing of petrol their visits once more became regular and Christopher Henham, in particular, always looked forward to slipping away on Friday evenings for a peaceful week end, which, to his constant surprise, he invariably managed to have.

In recent years however they had tended to keep much more to their own company and no longer was there the free and easy wandering in and out of each other's domains as had previously been the case. This was primarily due to two factors. One was that Celia didn't fit in, in the same way that Zena did; the other that, with his appointment as a judge, Gethin Riley now not only frequently treated his erstwhile colleagues with pontifical disdain from the rarified heights of the Bench but all too often assumed a similar attitude out of court.

Though Robin King-Selman had long since given up protesting that he much preferred to spend his week-ends in London, he had never accepted as valid the countless different reasons which his mother, with nimble ingenuity, always managed to think up for vetoing the idea. The truth was that, despite the fact it took him away from his laboratory and gave him two additional days a week in the company of his stepfather, he had come gradually to enjoy his week-ends at the cottage. It gave him time to think about other things and just recently he had had other things to think about. Maureen Fox was the first girl he had ever met whose presence gave him that sensation of butterflies in the stomach and an absurd constriction of the throat so that well-rehearsed phrases became still-born within the confines of his mind. If her presence succeeded in ravaging his equanimity, it was still, he felt, preferable to her absence, which, alas, was the far more common state. In any event these new sensations had given Robin cause to ponder.

It was Saturday morning and dressed in a pair of ancient grey flannels, a much too tight sports shirt and a once canary yellow pullover, he walked down the garden whistling thoughtfully and flung open the door of the toolshed to come face to face with Sir Gethin Riley.

'Oh – good morning, sir – er – I didn't know you were in here – you gave me quite a shock —' His voice gradually trailed away, as he stood abashed by the judge's silent and cobra-like stare.

'Good morning, young man', said Sir Gethin slowly, making the greeting sound as conventional as was possible. 'And what brings you to the toolshed? Not to tidy it up, of that I am quite sure.'

'Actually I was looking for the potassium cyanide.' Sir Gethin opened his eyes wide in surprise and Robin quickly added, 'There used to be some down here.'

'There still is.'

'We got it last summer to deal with those wasps' nests along the river bank.'

'We did', agreed Sir Gethin, still transfixing Robin with an unwavering stare.

'I thought I'd take some back to town, sir. I've run out', said Robin, persevering to make everything clear.

'Have you indeed? And how, may I ask, are you placed for arsenic, antimony, cantharidine and strychnine?' Robin laughed dutifully and Sir Gethin pointed to a small

29

tin on the top shelf which was boldly labelled POISON. 'There's the potassium cyanide and if you don't mind, I won't stay in the shed while you're dabbling with it. It's most dangerous stuff and if there's going to be a fatality I'd sooner neither be it nor witness it.' As he turned to go, the door opened and Helen stuck her head in.

'Oh, here you are, and Robin too. What have you been up to?' she asked, speaking to Robin.

'Nothing so far as I know.' He had no notion what she meant and added, 'Why?'

'A glossy car has just pulled up outside your front door and it looks to me suspiciously like a police one.'

'Oh.'

'I wonder what they can want', she said.

'And even supposing it is a police car, my dear, why should *you* do any wondering?' asked her husband, as he strolled out into the sunshine and gazed thoughtfully toward the Henhams' cottage. His wife followed him.

Left alone, Robin helped himself to the poison, putting some in a small test-tube, and returned to the house. As he reached the front door, a car pulled up and his father got out. Robin knew that he was expected for lunch, since he had been present when his mother and stepfather had discussed the matter and agreed that the invitation should be issued, as Christopher was due to play in an all-day golf competition and wouldn't be home till evening. Later when golf was out of the question because of his injured thumb, he had insisted with self-mocking chivalry that the arrangement should still stand and had said he would tactfully absent himself for the day.

'Hello, Robin', said Marcus King-Selman, eyeing the cottage after the manner of a sanitary inspector. 'What a charming little place it looks. You lead the way in.'

'Mummy, where are you? Father's arrived', Robin called out.

'I'm in here', replied Celia, looking up from her window-seat as they entered the lounge.

'What a glorious day I've brought with me', said her ex-husband with hearty cheerfulness as he greeted her with a one-cheek kiss. 'How's everything, old girl? I almost collided with some of your departing guests as I turned into the drive.'

'Yes, who were they?' broke in Robin. 'Lady Riley said they looked like police.'

'They were police', Celia replied.

'What on earth did they want?'

'They came to serve me with a summons.'

'What is it this time, Mummy?'

'This time it's manslaughter.'

CHAPTER FIVE

M ARCUS KING-SELMAN was the first to speak.
'Manslaughter? There must be some mistake. Are
you joking, Celia?'

In answer she handed him a piece of paper which she
had been holding. He took it from her and started to read
it, at first to himself, and then slowly aloud. '. . . Information has this day been laid before me the undersigned,
one of the Magistrates of the Magistrates' Courts of the
Metropolis sitting at West Central Magistrates' Court by
Detective-Sergeant Andrew Talper that you on the eighth
day of April 1954 in the Metropolitan Police District did
unlawfully kill Albert Toffee, against the peace of our
Sovereign Lady the Queen, her crown and dignity. You
are hereby summoned to appear —'

'Must you, Marcus?' said Celia suddenly. 'You make
it sound worse than the last judgment.'

'But, Mummy, what does it all mean?' asked Robin,
with a note of anguish in his voice.

'It means just what it says.'

'But who is this Toffee man?'

'I don't know who he *was*: only that I'm charged with
killing him.'

'And did you?' asked Marcus King-Selman. Celia
turned away and looked out of the window across the lawn
toward the river. 'Did you, Celia? You must answer.'

'If you'll both calm down a bit, I'll try and explain',
she said, turning back toward them. She hesitated a
moment and then added, 'At least I'm not sure that I can

explain anything yet. I think I must first consult Christopher.'

'But my dear Celia,' said her ex-husband in a voice louder than was necessary, 'this is a tremendously grave charge. It's next to murder. You can't just refuse to give us any explanation.'

'Next to murder', murmured Celia. 'I must say, darling, you manage to put things with stark simplicity but small tact.'

Robin had meanwhile sat down and was trying to read the summons which he had taken from his father's hand. His mind, however, refused to be concentrated on the grim words as he bit furiously on the stem of his unlit pipe. Marcus strode over to Celia and, pinioning her arms to her side, said:

'This is no time to swap small talk and comment on niceties of expression. I may be only your ex-husband but Robin is still your son and I consider that he, if not I, is entitled to know what has happened.' Celia shook herself free.

'I know you're both anxious on my behalf,' she said, 'and I suppose I must try and explain, though it won't be easy.'

'It's a charge of manslaughter, remember', Marcus said.

She seemed about to reply to this superfluous observation but then decided otherwise.

'This unfortunate man, Mr. Toffee, was knocked down by my car last Tuesday evening on the way back from Dick Lawford's cocktail-party. It seemed to be a very minor affair but apparently he has now died and I'm summoned for manslaughter.'

'But there must be more to it than that, Mummy. It can't be manslaughter if it wasn't your fault.'

'Obviously someone thinks it was.'

33

'You weren't tight, were you, Celia?'

'You saw me leave the party', she replied quickly. Marcus pursed his lips but said nothing.

'But, Mummy, you've never told me about being involved in any accident. Does my stepfather know about it?'

Celia sat down with a sigh.

'It's his accident', she said, and then went on to relate briefly what had happened. When she had finished she looked from one to the other of the two men. Robin was white and tense and Marcus looked extremely grim and very much like the traditional white man called to protect his womenfolk against assault by a band of orgiastic savages.

'Of course Henham will put this right as soon as he knows.' He said it as a statement of plain unarguable fact and clearly neither Celia nor Robin was expected to reply.

In the ten days which intervened between the issue of the summons and the date of its hearing, Celia often felt very much like a patient suffering from a grave illness on whose treatment the doctors were in quarrelsome disagreement. She had overcome her surprise (she didn't permit herself to use any word stronger than this when analysing her feelings about it) at her husband's first reaction and now pinned all her faith on the course he had prescribed.

On learning the news he had immediately put the matter in the hands of their family solicitor. Subsequently he had expressed considerable doubt at her wisdom in having told Marcus and Robin the truth and had insisted that there should be no further disclosure of it, not even to the solicitor. He constantly assured her that the charge of manslaughter would certainly be dismissed at the magistrates' court as it was quite apparent that the prosecution's evidence must fall far short of proving the very high degree

34

of negligent driving necessary to support it. He told her that this latter certainty was the one reason for maintaining the deception and had indicated some of the unpleasant consequences which would follow any divulgence of the truth to the police.

Thus Celia accepted the situation, realizing that not only was it one of her own contrivance but that, as her husband pointed out, to try to rectify it now would be to bring about the disasters which her initial deception had been designed to prevent.

On the evening before the court hearing they dined out alone and afterwards went to see a new Italian film at the Curzon. They got home about eleven and went straight up to bed.

'Well, this time tomorrow night it'll all be over', said Celia with a sigh, unzipping the side of her dress.

'I sincerely hope so.'

'Well, it will be, won't it, darling? You've been saying so all along.'

'In so far as anything is predictable it should be all right – absolutely all right.' After a pause he added, 'I think Butterworth's a good chap, don't you? You've got confidence in him?'

Butterworth was the solicitor who was being instructed to defend Celia. Their family solicitor's only experience of the criminal courts was confined to those rare occasions when his otherwise highly respectable clients got had up for minor peccadilloes. He would then rush round to his colleague, Mr. Butterworth, who was what is commonly called a police court solicitor, and whose professional ability he respected as much as he was jarred by his bursting confidence and natural ebullience. The family solicitor had been in favour of briefing counsel to appear in the magistrates' court but Christopher Henham had taken the line that the Butterworths of this world were far better equipped to handle the rough-and-tumble work involved in a police court hearing than were a great many counsel. Furthermore he had thought it would be a tactical error since the appearance of a well-known counsel in such a court often seemed to focus unwanted attention on his case and to put all others concerned with it very much on their guard. The family solicitor had bowed to these arguments but had not been able to help wondering to what extent they were prompted by thought of self.

'I think Mr. Butterworth is a sweetie', replied Celia. 'He said this afternoon that, if I've told him everything, he doesn't see how the prosecution can begin to make it a case of manslaughter and he thinks it's monstrous that they've brought the charge.' She sat on the edge of the bed and looked across at her husband, who was vigorously massaging his scalp. 'And I have told him everything, haven't I, darling?'

He stopped and came over to her. In a very gentle voice he said:

'You know how inexpressibly grateful I am to you, dearest one. You don't think I'd – I'd double-cross you and let you go on taking the blame if I wasn't sure about the outcome?'

'Of course I don't, darling. And I'm sorry I sounded such a doubting Thomas. It ought to be a doubting Thomasine or something, oughtn't it?'

'I swear that I've told you everything about the accident that human recollection can provide. You've passed it on to Butterworth as being of your own knowledge. Now he knows everything.' He got up and walked across to his dressing-room. As he passed through the doorway, he turned back and said, 'You don't mind my not coming to court with you in the morning, do you?'

'But of course not, darling. You're appearing in the Court of Appeal tomorrow, aren't you?'

'Yes, appealing against one of Gethin's judgments.'

'I shall be well looked after. Robin's coming with me and Marcus has insisted upon picking me up in a taxi just after ten.'

'I've arranged for Maureen Fox to be on tap, as well.' He took a step into his dressing-room and then, hesitating, turned back again. 'I'm sorry to say it again but I do wish you'd never told Robin or King-Selman. It *was* a mistake, you know. It's made *me* so terribly – vulnerable.'

Mr. Justice Riley did up the top button of his warm salmon-pink pyjamas and put on his dressing-gown. He studied himself for a moment in a full-length mirror and appeared well satisfied with what he saw. He squared his shoulders and reflected, not for the first time, how well a judge's scarlet and ermine robe suited him. Alas, it was one of life's minor frustrations that Her Majesty's Judges of the Probate, Divorce and Admiralty Division of the High Court of Justice wore an unglamorous black silk gown while their brethren of equal rank and pay of the Queen's Bench Division were clad in gorgeous, colourful scarlet when they tried the criminal cases which occupied so much of their time. Mr. Justice Riley had made it known in the right quarters that he would welcome a transfer, but so far nothing had happened and in the meantime he spent his days trying endless divorce cases robed in mournful black, and only had the satisfaction of appearing in his full scarlet and ermine outfit on a very restricted number of ceremonial occasions each year.

As he turned away from the mirror, his wife came in from the bathroom. Dressed in a shell pink négligée and with a peculiarly unbecoming sort of mob-cap pulled down over her head she appeared to be of almost doll-like proportions.

'You've come to bed very early this evening', she said.

'I've had a tiring day. Two dreadful asses before me who seemed determined to exasperate me as much as they could.'

'Who were they?'

'A middle-aged junior named Brent and an almost briefless Queen's Counsel of the name of Silliken.'

'I thought Brent was supposed to be rather able.'

'He showed a vast lack of any ability to-day.' Sir Gethin sat down on his bed and started to clip his toenails.

'Not all over the carpet, Gethin', cried Helen through a generous layer of cold cream.

Her husband took no notice of this *cri de cœur* but continued with his task. 'Doesn't Celia Henham appear before a court tomorrow?' he asked.

'Yes', said Helen crossly, watching bits of toenail fly about the room. 'I should think she'll be glad when the day's over.'

'I don't see why she should be. Tomorrow is only the beginning of her troubles.'

'But Christopher says the magistrate can't possibly commit her for trial. He says the prosecution's evidence is terribly thin.'

'Christopher would appear to be, what is called, whistling in the dark. Either that or he is exhibiting his well-known penchant for injudicious forecasts.' As he spoke, he snipped fiercely at a horny toenail, then in an unctuous tone he added, 'Anyway, we shall see. But the whole affair cannot fail to react unfavourably on his practice and career.' He looked up as he finished speaking just in time to catch his wife's expression in the dressing-table mirror. It was an expression blended of fright and dislike; but exactly what she was frightened of and whom she disliked, Mr. Justice Riley didn't bother to pursue.

CHAPTER SIX

M AUREEN FOX had never before been inside one of the Metropolitan Magistrates' Courts. None of the members of the select Chambers to which she belonged had any criminal practice to speak of, except Mr. Peckles. He was something of a lone wolf (albeit an extremely affable one) and spent his life cheerfully chasing from County Court to Magistrates' Court to Quarter Sessions and back again, thereby earning a very large number of three- and five-guinea fees in the course of a year—infinitely more, in fact, than many who liked to talk to him in condescending tones of their High Court practices.

Maureen got off a bus and asked the way to the court. When she reached the top of the road in which it was supposed to be, she looked doubtfully down at a milling scene of street traders and urchin footballers. The shrill, raucous and unintelligible cries of the former mingled with the non-stop babble of the latter. From time to time the two factions turned on each other, as when a football landed smartly on a barrow and dislodged a crate of cabbages or made even flatter an undernourished plaice.

Maureen approached a large pregnant blonde woman who was wheeling a pram which contained three visible children, with the promise of others out of sight.

'Excuse me, but could you please tell me where West Central Magistrates' Court is?'

'Down there, ducks — See', she said, pointing at a

39

building about one hundred yards down on the right-hand side. 'That one with the pole on top.'

'Thank you so much.'

'Pleasure, ducks. Not in trouble, I hope.'

'Not to-day,' said Maureen with a laugh and then added, 'so far.'

The fat blonde let forth a gale of laughter and a hidden child stirred uneasily in the pram.

Maureen picked her way gingerly down the street, keeping a wary eye both on the footballers and on the cods' heads, squashed tomatoes and wizened sprouts which littered her path. She reached the court unscathed and went in. The entrance hall was large, bare and drab and on narrow benches round its walls sat a cross-section of the community. Their only common quality seemed to be a lack of cheerfulness. Some looked apprehensive (probably with excellent reason, thought Maureen) and others stolid and bemused. None looked happy. She studied a long list which was in a glass case on the wall and saw that 'Celia Henham: manslaughter: Det.-Sgt. Talper' was the only case under the heading 'SUMMONSES 11 a.m.' It was the last entry on the list and above it, under the respective headings of 'Charges' and 'Remands', were some twenty-five names whose trouble seemed to vary from prostitution to procuration and from assault to abortion.

It seemed to Maureen as she looked around that she had never seen so many doors leading off a hall before. Feeling rather like Alice in one of her hot pursuits after the White Rabbit she started to study the signs on each. 'Warrant Office', 'Probation Officer', 'MEN' (it appeared that the needs of 'GENTLEmen' were not catered for at West Central Court). There followed 'Barristers and Solicitors', 'Press', 'Private', 'Court – Witnesses and Advocates' and 'Keep Out'. She approached the Witnesses' and Advocates' door and explained her mission to the police officer who had immediately tried to bar her way. Without comment he indicated a space on a hard bench in front of the public standing room and she went and sat down.

Mr. Cathie, the magistrate, had just taken his seat and the first offender was stumbling into the ridiculous little dock. The court itself immediately reminded Maureen of a cattle market, being made up of small pens in which over-large people were now trying to fit themselves with the minimum of discomfort. She turned her gaze on Mr. Cathie. He was bald and had a large, round, beaming face. She reckoned that he must be extremely short and he looked just like a benign Humpty-Dumpty.

The first eight people with whom he dealt were all charged with drunkenness and they followed one another in and out of the dock with kaleidoscopic effect. Several of them were clearly highly respectable businessmen who had overcelebrated the previous evening and whose melancholic airs were born of a blend of natural hangover and of genuine mortification at their predicament. Each probably longed to be quietly soothed by Alka-Seltzer and a sympathetic secretary and fervently hoped that no word of their appearance in court would filter through to their staid relations. Mr. Cathie beamed at them all and his 'Pay ten shillings if you please' was said with such charm as to make it scarcely sound like the imposition of a fine.

The straightforward drunks were succeeded by two hoary old customers of the court who were charged with being drunk and disorderly. The first was a huge bearded man who looked as though he'd come straight from a Canadian lumber camp. He and Mr. Cathie seemed delighted to see each other again and their mutual pleasure seemed to be quite unclouded by Mr. Cathie saying, 'I think it had better be twenty-eight days this time. Thank you, next case, please.' The bearded giant

41

went happily on his way to the cells and was followed by an exceedingly prim-looking old lady who, it appeared, had insisted upon snuggling down to rest on a zebra crossing and showing strong resentment at the efforts of a young police constable to remove her.

'Tut, tut', said Mr. Cathie, still beaming as the story was unfolded.

'– lies', said the prim old lady on being asked what she would like to say. Mr. Cathie pursed his lips and sighed.

'Ah well, we haven't had the pleasure of your company for some weeks. I think forty shillings or seven days this time, if you please.'

And so they followed each other in and out of the dock with a practised rhythm and eleven o'clock came and went. Mr. Cathie never stopped beaming and never looked ruffled and Maureen came to recognize the sorrowful shake of his head which inevitably presaged a sentence of imprisonment. At last all the charges and remands were disposed of and the court gaoler was relieved by the warrant-officer who was responsible for Summonses and who now went into the hall and called to Celia, who was waiting there with her escorts.

'Mrs. Henham? This way please, madam.'

Celia had given considerable thought to her dress for the occasion and now took her place in front of the dock attired in respectful grey and a pair of sun spectacles. She felt that the latter would serve two desirable purposes: one to excite a certain sympathy in those who were about to decide her future; the other, more utilitarian and certainly better founded, namely to be able to stare, study or sleep without obviously doing any of these things.

Mr. Cathie motioned her to sit down and she did so with a graceful inclination of the head, looking ridiculously like Gainsborough's famous lady acknowledging a greeting from the head gamekeeper.

Mr. Butterworth sat at a table in the pen just in front of her which was reserved for solicitors. At least every other minute he turned round, apparently to make sure she was still bearing up. Celia felt that the moment would shortly come when he would suggest a rug over her knees or an arrowroot biscuit. Behind her, on the same bench as Maureen, sat Marcus and Robin. The latter was doing much whispering to Maureen but Marcus looked as severe and forbidding as a battle-thwarted General.

'Yes, Mr. Lilyman', said Mr. Cathie when everyone was seated and the curtain was ready to be rung up. Mr. Lilyman had already attracted Celia's attention and it came as rather a shock to her that such a pleasant and self-possessed-looking young man should be the person deputed to prosecute her. He sat over to her right in yet another pen, that reserved for barristers, and rose to his feet at the magistrate's cue. As he did so he gave Celia a mild, appraising glance and she winked at him from behind her sun spectacles. Either he was even more self-possessed than he looked or the spectacles more effective than Celia supposed, for he showed no sign of being disconcerted but, turning to Mr. Cathie, began his opening speech.

'May it please you, sir, I appear in this case on behalf of the Director of Public Prosecutions and the defendant, Mrs. Celia Henham, is represented by my friend, Mr. Butterworth' – he wasn't really his friend and they had never met before, but thus the traditional way in which advocates refer to each other in court. He paused and slowly took off his newly acquired spectacles which had added so enormously to his repertoire of forensic tricks. 'She comes before you, sir, charged with the manslaughter of Albert Toffee on the eighth of April this year. Mr.

Toffee was sixty-three years old and a confectionery consultant at the time of his death.'

'A what?' Mr. Cathie asked as Mr. Lilyman had hoped he would. Alas, however, the little joke he had prepared was stillborn since the magistrate quickly added, 'Anyway, I don't suppose it has any relevance to the charge. Yes, go on, Mr. Lilyman.'

'About ten-twenty on that evening he was cycling home along Gloucester Road, as was his custom, when he was struck by a car driven by Mrs. Henham and as a result of injuries which he thereby sustained, he died in hospital some thirty-six hours later.' Mr. Lilyman paused, swept the court with a pleased look and then said with great deliberation, 'The car driven by Mrs. Henham failed to stop after the accident though, in the prosecution's submission, it must have been apparent to her that she had been involved in one in which this cyclist had sustained at least some personal injury – if nothing worse, as has turned out to be the case.' Celia gave an involuntary shudder and decided that Mr. Lilyman's outward appearance was a grossly deceptive one. Her sombre dress and sympathy-exciting sun spectacles were having no effect on him at all. 'Fortunately,' Mr. Lilyman went on, 'a witness took the number of the car and later that evening Police Constables Long and Bright called at Mrs. Henham's house and she at once admitted being the driver of the car and her awareness of having been involved in this accident. She offered, however, no explanation to the officers for not having stopped.' Celia shot Mr. Lilyman a look of cordial dislike. What he had just said was a grossly unfair distortion of fact. Neither of the officers had asked her for any such explanation. 'The officers examined the car, a Rover, registered number ZIZ 919 and found slight damage to the nearside front wing, indicative of a recent accident.' This time Mr. Lilyman slowed up while adjusting his spectacles further up the bridge of his nose. 'The evidence makes it clear, sir, that this car only just touched Mr. Toffee on his bicycle and that at the time he was riding on his correct side of the road about eighteen inches from the kerb and was showing proper lights. But why did the car touch Mr. Toffee at all?' asked Mr. Lilyman rhetorically. 'The answer, sir, lies in the evidence of the witness who took the number of the car and who will tell you that in his view, it was being driven at an excessive speed and in a thoroughly erratic manner.' Celia, as she listened to this unpleasant recital of events for the first time, began to wonder if everything was really going to go according to plan. However at that moment Mr. Butterworth turned round and gave her a look as reassuring as the Rock of Gibraltar and she felt better again. But excessive speed and erratic driving were developments as unexpected as they were unwelcome. She took a quick glance behind her and saw that Marcus's features were set in granite grimness and Robin was still whispering to Maureen. 'The evidence of that witness will be supported by another who saw this car being driven along the road about two hundred yards before the accident and whose attention to it was attracted solely by its speed and the general manner in which it was being driven.' Mr. Lilyman paused and thoughtfully removed his spectacles whose frames seemed likely to wear out long before the lenses. 'That, sir, is a brief outline of the evidence in this case and the allegation which the prosecution makes is that this unfortunate man, Albert Toffee, lost his life as a direct result of the manner in which the defendant was driving her car that night – a manner so grossly negligent as to make this a case of manslaughter. If the evidence inclines you to the same view, sir, then I shall in due course ask for a committal for trial at the Central Criminal Court.'

'Skates over the law the way they always do', murmured Mr. Butterworth in an aside which all could, and
were intended to, hear. 'He'll have to do better than that
for manslaughter and I don't doubt that his witnesses
won't even support what he has said. They always open
high and woolly, when their evidence is thin. Just wait till
we throw Bateman's and Andrews' cases at him. They're
the law of England on degree of negligence in motoring
cases, not his airy-fairy generalities.' At almost every
conference Celia had had with him, Mr. Butterworth had
talked about the cases of *R.* v. *Bateman* and *Andrews* v.
D.P.P. and she had come to regard them as faithful
friends of his and *ipso facto* stout allies of hers. Their
formidable strength was symbolized in the two solid tomes
which stood on the table in front of the solicitor, who now
demonstrated his scorn of Mr. Lilyman's assault by
ostentatiously turning their pages. This was part of the
cold war of *Regina* against *Henham*.

Mr. Lilyman's first witness was the pathologist who had
conducted a post-mortem examination on the body of
Albert Toffee. He hurried into the witness-box, took the
oath in tones of brisk authority and gave his evidence in
the manner of a sorely tried teacher lecturing a class of
backward children. Mr. Lilyman just stood and gave the
doctor an occasional encouraging, but in the circumstances quite unnecessary nod. It seemed that Mr. Toffee
had died as a result of a fractured skull and a contused
brain and that these injuries were consistent with his
having been knocked off his bicycle and his head having
struck the hard surface of the road. Celia, who had listened
abstractedly to this evidence, was far more impressed at
the speed with which the clerk wrote it all down in long-
hand, his pen dancing over the sheets of paper like a
will-o'-the-wisp. On its conclusion it was read back to
the doctor, who signed it as being a true deposition of

what he had said and then departed on his daily round of courts and mortuaries. To Celia's surprise, Mr. Butterworth had asked the doctor no questions in cross-examination; but she had nevertheless been impressed by the effect he managed to convey even in such negative conduct.

The pathologist was followed into the witness-box by a police constable who produced a plan of the scene of the accident, and he in turn made way for another officer who produced an album of photographs which he had taken at the same place. Celia glanced over Mr. Butterworth's shoulder at his copy of the photographs and found it impossible to regard pictures of such an ordinary street with its shops, bus stops and gawking bystanders as the scene of a crime – her alleged crime of homicide. She sat back against the rails of the dock and watched the next witness make his way to the witness-box. He was a middle-aged man with a thin and bitter face. He looked as though he resented everything about Mr. Cathie's court and as he reached the box his eyes darted with suspicion and truculence, like the tongue of a venomous snake. When he had taken the oath, Mr. Lilyman gave him a warming smile which was intended to win his confidence and put him at his ease. It achieved neither but merely seemed to increase his suspicion.

'Is your name Bartholomew Bufton?'

'Yes, it is.'

'And do you live at 84, Lansbury Buildings, W.14?'

'Yes, I do.'

'And what is your occupation, Mr. Bufton?'

'You've got it there', Mr. Bufton replied, nodding at the statement which Mr. Lilyman held in his hand.

'Yes I know, Mr. Bufton, but would you please tell the court what you do for a living?'

'I works for the L.C.C.' The reply was accompanied by a look of clear warning to Mr. Lilyman not to proceed further with this particular line of questioning. Mr. Lilyman sighed but supposed he couldn't really blame Mr. Bufton for not admitting to the honourable occupation of public lavatory attendant.

'About 10.20 p.m. on Tuesday, 8th April this year, were you walking along Gloucester Road?'

Mr. Bufton nodded.

'Yes or no?' asked the clerk with asperity. 'I can't write down nods.'

Mr. Bufton glared at him. 'Yes', he said grudgingly.

'And what did you see?' asked Mr. Lilyman.

'I've told the police once. You've got it all wrote down there in my statement.'

'True', said Mr. Lilyman, unperturbed and quite used to recalcitrant witnesses. 'But I'm afraid you now have to tell us again. Remember you're on oath this time and the learned clerk is writing down your evidence.'

'What d'you mean about me being on oath this time? D'you think I didn't tell the police the truth? Because if that's the way —'

'Now stop being argumentative and behave yourself', broke in Mr. Cathie. 'Just answer counsel's questions and we'll get along much quicker.'

'Well, what was it you saw happen?' Mr. Lilyman asked again.

'Lots of things', said Mr. Bufton sulkily.

'That's quite enough of that.' This time Mr. Cathie spoke even more energetically. 'If you don't behave yourself you'll go and cool your heels in a cell. Contempt of court, Mr. Bufton: that's what it's called and that's where it'll lead you.'

'Well?'

'I saw this car hit this cyclist.'

'What sort of car?'

'A green saloon.'

'Did you notice its number?'

'You know I did.'

'What was it?' asked Mr. Lilyman quickly, wishing to avoid a further contretemps and the possible removal from court of his most important witness.

'ZIZ 919.'

'Could you recognize the driver?'

'Never saw the driver at all. Only noticed the car after it had passed me. How could I see the driver?'

'Whereabouts was the cyclist when you saw the car strike him?'

'About a foot from the kerb.'

'Which kerb?' 'Going in which direction?' 'How fast?' So the questions inexorably followed one another until all Mr. Bufton's evidence was eventually prised out of him and he was allowed to stand down and take a seat at the back of the court. Despite his hostility to all and sundry (he had obviously disliked Mr. Butterworth as much as anyone else) he had come up to proof and there was little in his evidence to comfort Celia or her advisers.

His place in the witness-box was taken by a well-set-up young woman who turned out to be a games mistress by the name of Hilda Cook. It was she who had seen the car about two hundred yards short of the accident. She answered all Mr. Lilyman's questions with admirable clarity and conciseness and then turned a look of quizzical interest on to Mr. Butterworth as he rose to cross-examine her.

'You estimate the speed of the car as having been about forty-five miles an hour, is that right, Miss Cook?' he asked, after a number of other questions.

'About that, yes. I'm not an expert judge of speed —'

'Do you wish to change your evidence about it now?'

'Certainly not. I said about forty-five. If it was more or less, it was still in my view too fast.'

Mr. Butterworth pursed his lips and then in a distinctly acid tone asked, 'You don't drive a car yourself, do you, Miss Cook?'

'No.'

'I thought not', he said in a forensic aside which brought Mr. Lilyman to his feet.

'I must ask my friend to refrain from commenting on the evidence in the course of cross-examination. It is most improper.'

'Yes, very well. Go on with your questions, Mr. Butterworth and remember that I am not a jury', said Mr. Cathie.

'And you're a schoolteacher, Miss Cook?' continued Mr. Butterworth.

'Yes.'

'And all schoolteachers are nowadays very much occupied in instilling road safety measures into their pupils?'

'Yes, we try to do that.'

'Would it be fair to describe you as anti motorist?'

'I'm anti bad driving', replied Miss Cook in a challenging tone.

'Ah.' Mr. Butterworth managed to convey a wealth of comment with this monosyllable. 'Do you see a great deal of what *you* consider to be bad driving?'

'A very great deal, unfortunately.'

'But you've never owned nor driven a car yourself?'

It might perhaps have been more prudent of Mr. Butterworth to have sat down while this question still hung in the air unanswered. But as so often is the case, the urge to stay on one's feet becomes a wellnigh irresistible one to many advocates, though invariably to their own undoing and that of their hapless clients.

'No I haven't; but I often travel in cars and I think I'm as good as the next person at recognizing bad driving when I see it. As I've said, it wasn't only the speed of this car which attracted my attention but the way in which it was swerving about slightly. I can only repeat —'

'It's quite all right, Miss Cook', Mr. Butterworth broke in petulantly. 'We don't want to hear it all over again.' At this, Mr. Cathie beamed serenely at the ceiling and Mr. Lilyman didn't bother to hide his own amusement. After a few more questions in an endeavour to restore the situation, Mr. Butterworth sat down.

It was just five minutes past one when the last witness signed his deposition and Mr. Lilyman announced that that was the case for the prosecution. Immediately Mr. Butterworth sprang to his feet and said that he wished to make a submission. Mr. Cathie looked at the clock and then back at Mr. Butterworth with a resigned expression.

'Yes, very well', he said.

The submission was the usual one in such circumstances, namely that the evidence for the prosecution did not disclose a prima facie case and that his client should not be committed for trial before a judge and jury, but that the charge should then and there be dismissed. There was no gainsaying the eloquence of his plea. He first dealt with the facts of the case and poured scorn upon the evidence of Mr. Bufton and Miss Cook, asserting with confidence that no jury could possibly accept what they had said. He magnanimously added that he had no doubt they were sincere in their belief of what they thought they'd seen, but their unreliability as witnesses had been amply demonstrated by his cross-examination. Thus went the submission. Later he turned to the law and, like Aladdin, summoned to his aid the legal judgments in the cases of Messrs. Bateman and Andrews. Finally, hoarse and perspiring, he sat down.

Even as he did so, Mr. Cathie, in a quiet and calm voice, said, 'I'm satisfied that there is a case to answer and evidence to go before a jury on this charge.'

Celia, dazed by the suddenness with which the climax had been reached, was bidden to stand and after a rigmarole of legal formulae had been recited at her, Mr. Cathie, looking with a sigh at the clock, said, 'Celia Henham, you are committed to take your trial at the next session of the Central Criminal Court upon this charge of manslaughter.'

Five minutes later, still dazed and now bailed, Celia stood on the pavement outside the court with Marcus and Robin. None of them said anything until they were settled back in a taxi.

'Don't worry', said Marcus. 'I'll see Henham about this.'

Celia shook her head.

'Let's stop and have a drink', she said. 'We'll be able to think more calmly then.'

CHAPTER SEVEN

Maureen fox had phoned through the news to Chambers before leaving the Magistrates' Court, but as soon as she got back to the Temple, Alfred Exley told her that Christopher Henham wanted an immediate first-hand account from her.

She found him pacing up and down his room in obvious perturbation and as she entered he came across and caught her by the wrist with his free hand, his left arm still being in a sling.

'This is terrible, Maureen. I simply can't understand it. What on earth happened? What went wrong? Did Butterworth foozle the case or what?'

He sat down in the deep leather arm-chair and motioned her to be seated as well. She did so on the edge of the desk and then related the whole morning's proceedings to the best of her recollection. He listened almost without interruption until she had finished and then said with a good deal of vehemence:

'The trouble is some of these magistrates just regard themselves as rubber stamps in committal for trial cases; there to approve any course the prosecution propose. It really is monstrous; especially considering the more than adequate salaries they get. It's nothing more nor less than an abnegation of their proper judicial function.'

Maureen, who had been considerably impressed by Mr. Cathie and the way he ran his court and who not very long ago had heard Christopher Henham hold forth on the pitiful salaries paid to stipendiary magistrates, decided that this was not the moment to mention either matter.

'But even though your wife has been committed for trial, there's surely still every reason to expect she'll be acquitted, isn't there?' she asked.

'Acquitted', he said bitterly. 'Acquitted she may be but not without my crucifixion.'

'I don't understand.'

'Don't try to, my dear. I'm being stupidly melodramatic.'

'Isn't there something I can do to help, Mr. Henham?' she asked tenderly, with a slight catch in her voice. It was the first time she had ever seen him in a position where such an offer was possible and she coloured as she spoke.

'Yes, get me Lady Riley on the phone, will you?'

Whether or not he had deliberately misunderstood her didn't seem to matter to Maureen as she left his room. What did matter to her for the moment was that she had met with a rebuff which left her mind smarting and her cheeks burning.

Celia and Christopher dined at home alone that evening. She had expected him to ply her with questions about the court hearing as soon as he returned, but, apart from a brief expression of sympathy accompanied by a kiss, he had made no further reference to what had happened and it was Celia who had at last given him a long, unsolicited account of the day's events. He had listened to this in polite silence and had answered the various questions, with which she interspersed her narrative, in economic monosyllables. Finally he had told her that the best-laid plans sometimes went astray and she wasn't to worry unduly as everything would still be all right.

She was, however, both puzzled and a little aggrieved by his obvious reluctance to discuss her predicament. It was, after all, he who had fairly and squarely landed her in it. At least, her own impetuously generous nature was partly to blame, she supposed, though her husband had shown little chivalry in his acceptance and exploitation of her original gesture. These and other thoughts passed through her mind as she watched him finish his meal.

'Perhaps we could go to a film, darling. I'll just wash up these things first.'

'Where's Doris?' he asked, referring to their moon-faced maid of all work.

'She's gone off to bury her uncle.'

'Why?'

'I suppose he must have died', Celia replied vaguely. 'But it won't take me long and I'll bring you some coffee while I'm doing it.'

'I'm afraid I can't go out this evening, sweetheart. I've got someone coming to see me at nine.'

'Oh, what a curse! And I felt just in the mood for a film. Can't you possibly put him off? Tell him your wife has got mumps or something.'

'I'm afraid I can't', he said, shaking his head.

'Who is it? Anyone I know?'

'No. It's just a small business matter I've got to discuss', he replied in the tone often used by husbands to cut short their wives' questions. 'But I'll get it through as quickly as possible and perhaps we could go out afterwards. He should be here any time now', he added, looking at his watch.

Five minutes later when the front-door bell rang, he gave Celia no chance to satisfy her curiosity but bounded from the room, and all she could hear were conventional greetings in the hall before the study door closed.

. . . . .

'It's very good of you to come along, Superintendent', said Christopher Henham after he had given his visitor a chair. 'Let me get you a drink. Whisky and soda?'

'Beer if you have it, sir', replied Detective-Superintendent Simon Manton. 'I hope I can help you, but officially, you understand, your wife's case is none of my business.'

'No, I appreciate that, but as you'll shortly see, I'm in a fearful fix and I felt as a first step that I'd rather discuss it unofficially with someone I knew at the Yard than make any official approach.' He handed Manton a glass of beer and put the bottle on the table beside him. After helping himself to a whisky and soda, he sat down behind his desk. 'I don't know how much of the story you know, Superintendent', he said, leaning forward and clasping his hands together on top of the desk.

'After you'd phoned me, sir, I got in touch with Detective-Sergeant Talper, who is the officer in charge of the case and whom I know well, and I've been along and had a look at our file.' He noticed the look on Christopher's face and added, 'I didn't mention to Talper the reason I was interested in the case.'

Christopher took a deep breath and, focusing his gaze on Manton, said:

'I won't beat about the bush, Superintendent, the position is simply this. The charge against my wife is an utterly false one. False not through any fault of the police or their witnesses, but on account of an uncontrolled march of events for which I accept full responsibility. Heaven alone knows what criminal offences I've committed.' He paused for a moment. 'You see, my wife wasn't driving at all that night; it was I who was driving her car.'

Beyond an expression of bright and intelligent interest, Manton showed no emotion at all as Christopher Henham went on to tell the whole story, which began with Celia's quixotic act of false confession.

'That's the whole of it, Superintendent', he said finally. 'I'm only too well aware that I've rendered myself liable to all sorts of criminal charges, ruined my career and destroyed my social position, but I can't possibly let the matter go any further. The question is what to do? If I go to the police officially and tell them all I've just told you, I suppose the Director of Public Prosecutions could get the Attorney-General to enter a *nolle presequi* when my wife comes up for trial and then you can go against me for manslaughter, public mischief and a host of kindred crimes. What do you advise, Superintendent?'

Manton looked thoughtful for a few moments and then said slowly:

'In the first place, sir, you've got to persuade the police of the truth of your story.'

'What do you mean?' asked Christopher, a trifle testily.

'It's not going to be easy, after all this time and after a full magisterial hearing followed by a committal for trial, to persuade them that your wife has silently taken the blame and that you have silently acquiesced in her so doing.'

'But I've explained all that', he said, a note of exasperation creeping into his voice. 'You believe me, don't you, Superintendent?'

'It doesn't matter whether I believe you or not, sir. All I say is that you won't find it an easy job and that's something of an understatement. There are too many points of evidence against her.'

'Such as? Give me one single item more consistent with my wife having driven the car than myself.'

'Very well, sir. The position of the driving seat.'

'But don't you see, Superintendent. That's exactly why I was driving erratically', replied Christopher in a half-pitying tone after a moment's pause. 'Not only had I sprained my thumb that evening – as you can see I've now got the wretched thing in a sling – but I hadn't bothered to adjust the seat when I took the car from the party. Don't those two things together perfectly well account for a piece of bad driving?'

'They could do perhaps, sir.'

'There you are then', he said triumphantly. 'Any other single item more consistent with my wife having been the driver rather than I?'

'Only the total improbability of your story, sir. Even if you can persuade the powers that be that your wife is the sort of person who says she's been involved in a motor accident when she hasn't, you'll never get them to believe your story of the gross deception which followed.' He paused and fixed Christopher with his bright blue eyes. 'You see, sir, they'll listen to you politely and then remark that Mr. Christopher Henham is not only a renowned Queen's Counsel but a gentleman of unusual chivalry as well.'

'Is that what you believe? That I'm doing this out of a sense of chivalry?'

'It doesn't matter what I believe, sir.'

About the time that Detective-Superintendent Manton left the Henhams' house, Maureen Fox was trying for the umpteenth time to disengage her hand from the moist grip of Robin's as they sat together in the Luxus Cinema. It was a 3D film with super-stereophonic sound and the atmosphere was anything but conducive to making love, which was Robin's chief purpose. There was no doubt in his mind that the days of silent films, when the only sound came from the indefatigable pianist beneath the palm fronds in the orchestra pit, must have been infinitely more propitious to that end.

Almost before Maureen had time to flex her cramped fingers, Robin's warm questing hand was feeling her left knee. She pushed it away.

'Stop it, Robin', she said, a trifle irritably.

'Why? Don't you like it?' He sounded hurt.

'You want to learn some technique.' It was an unkind thing to say and a moment later she went on, 'Oh, let's go. I'm fed up with this picture.' As she spoke a character on the screen hurled a Ming vase and she ducked with the result that their heads bumped and Robin seized the opportunity of giving her an ardent but clumsy kiss.

As they walked away from the cinema, Robin broke the silence.

'You're in a funny mood this evening, Maureen. What's wrong? Is it something I've said or done?'

'All you boys are the same. You seem to think that all a girl is interested in is a lot of crude necking. You're just a lot of animals, that's what you are.'

'Well, what does a girl want?'

'Not that. Anyway, I don't.'

'I suppose you prefer the older types', he said, nettled.

'Meaning?'

'Like my stepfather for instance. The sophisticated lady-slayer type.'

Maureen flushed and her eyes glinted with annoyance.

'Well, if you really want to know, you could certainly learn a thing or two from him.'

'Probably, though I cannot see why so many women – including my mother – are taken in by all that superficial charm. I know you are and it's you who'll end up by being hurt.'

'I'm quite capable of looking after myself, thank you very much', Maureen said coldly. 'Here's my bus, so

I'll say good night.' She swung on to it as she spoke and it drew away from the kerb. All the way home she pondered the evening's events. Somehow everything had gone wrong and she realized that her own mood was largely responsible for the unsatisfactory time she and Robin had just spent together. Even then he had no right to make such spiteful remarks about his stepfather. Sophisticated lady-slayer indeed. He had more technique of tender love-making in the tip of his little finger than Robin had in the whole of his body and to call his charm superficial was sheer envy.

At twenty minutes past four on the following afternoon Christopher Henham walked along one of the private corridors which run behind the courtrooms of the Royal Courts of Justice. He stopped outside a door, on the wall beside which was painted 'Mr. Justice Riley', and knocked.

'Come in.' He entered. 'Hullo, Christopher, have a chair and make yourself at home. Even suck one of your cough sweets if you want to.'

'Mine are not suckable like yours, Gethin', replied Christopher, deciding to acknowledge the gibe. 'I must say that I've always thought that the manufacturers of Umujubes and similar medicinal lollipops would be in Carey Street but for the Bench of England. Their annual consumption must be astronomical and I've often wondered which judge it was who first set the fashion.'

'Mm', said Mr. Justice Riley, who never liked any sort of counter-attack to his sallies. 'Very interesting, but I don't suppose you wanted to see me to discuss cough lozenges.'

'It's about Celia, Gethin.'

'She comes up at the next Old Bailey session, doesn't she?'

'Yes, and if something is not done soon, there'll be a ghastly miscarriage of justice. In fact there has been already; she should never have been committed for trial.'

'Cathie's a very able and experienced magistrate', commented the judge.

'That wasn't quite what I meant.' If I'm not careful Gethin will provoke me into saying something better left unsaid, thought Christopher Henham. Aloud he went on, 'The point is that I should be in the dock and not Celia.'

'And why do you say that?'

'Because I was driving the car at the time and not she. I'd better explain from the beginning.'

Sir Gethin Riley listened in silence, rather as he might to a bad plea in his court and, when it was finished, said, 'And in what way is it that you think I can help you?'

'The police won't believe my story unless I can offer them some corroboration of it.'

'Well?'

'There *is* someone who could support my word and thereby ensure Celia's acquittal.'

'Me?' asked the judge, with a faintly sarcastic smile.

'No, your wife.'

'Helen?'

'Yes, she was with me at the time of the accident. We'd met at Lawford's cocktail-party and I was giving her a lift afterwards.'

'And why have I been told nothing of this before?'

'We – I thought the case against Celia would be dismissed at the Magistrates' Court, in which event there was no point in worrying more people than necessary.'

'But things not having turned out as you expected, you now wish to embroil me in the odious deception which you've perpetrated; is that it?'

'No, it isn't, Gethin, and you know damned well it isn't. I simply want you to tell Helen that she must support my story and make the necessary statement to the police to the effect that I was the driver. It can't possibly do her or you any harm.'

'You really think that?' said Sir Gethin sharply and then added, 'But you always have had some incredible blind spots in your make-up. However, have you spoken to Helen yourself?'

'I have and she refuses.'

'For what reason?'

'The scandal involved.'

'Of course, even if Helen did do what you want – support your story, true or false – there's still no guarantee that the police would believe it.'

'They'd have to.'

'I don't think so. I suppose you haven't mentioned her name to them?'

'No. Not yet.'

'Not yet – I see. But if Helen continues to refuse to say what you want, then you will drag her in regardless.'

'You're doing your best to make it sound like blackmail, Gethin. It's nothing of the sort. My only concern is to clear Celia of a false charge. I don't care what happens to myself.'

'Nor to anyone else, it appears.'

'Nothing much can happen to anyone else.'

'Just now it was nothing at all could.'

'For heaven's sake, Gethin, don't be so intent on picking a quarrel. You must see that I had to come to you, because you're the only person who can make Helen see where her duty lies.'

'When is the next Old Bailey session?'

'In two weeks' time.'

'Very well, I'll let you have my decision in due course and now if you will excuse me —'

Christopher got up with a sigh and crossed to the door.

He stopped for a moment with his hand on the handle and then with a slight shrug of the shoulders opened it. He turned back toward the squat figure of Mr. Justice Riley sitting behind his desk.

'You're making it very difficult for me, Gethin, but I'd like your decision, as you call it, as soon as possible. There's a lot to be done. Good night.' The judge, who appeared to be staring right through him as he spoke, absent-mindedly helped himself to an Umujube as the door closed.

CHAPTER EIGHT

THE divorce case of Luce against Luce in which Christopher Henham was briefed to appear for the world-renowned actor, Godfrey Luce, was due to be tried at the Law Courts by Mr. Justice Riley about one week before Celia was destined to stand her trial about a mile further east at the Old Bailey.

Christopher's preparation of the case was not assisted by the various matters which weighed upon his mind and to which there had been a recent and embarrassingly troublesome addition.

One evening a few days before the case was due to be heard, he sent for his clerk.

'Alfred, I want to have a word with you about Maureen', he said. 'She will have to go.'

'Go, sir?'

'I'm afraid so. It'll be better for her in the long run.'

'But she's extremely efficient and it'll be very difficult to replace her.'

'My reasons have nothing to do with her efficiency. We'll just have to find someone else and train them to our ways and traditions.'

Alfred Exley, who never said a great deal and who, like most barrister's clerks, kept his eyes well skinned and always had one ear (if not both at once) trained to the ground, was not as surprised by this demand for Maureen's dismissal as he might have been.

'Shall you speak to her, sir?'

'No, Alfred, and I would sooner you didn't mention me when you give her notice. Be as nice as you can about it. She'd better go by the end of next week.'

And with that their conversation on the subject ended and Alfred Exley went home to ponder how the matter could best be broken to Maureen. He was considerably disturbed and did not at all relish what he had to do. In fact he greatly dreaded Maureen's reaction to the news.

Two days later, on the evening before the divorce case was due to start, Christopher and Helen sat in a small discreetly-lit booth of the Mayfair bar which had become their permanent rendezvous. Their conversation was a repetition of that which had taken place between them on numerous previous occasions in the past ten days.

'I wish you wouldn't worry so much, Christopher. It's quite unnecessary. You know Celia is bound to get off.'

'But supposing she doesn't?'

'She'd never go to prison anyway.'

'How can you talk like that, Helen?'

'Try and view the whole thing calmly. Celia has taken the blame for this accident because she is a devoted wife and has a quixotically generous nature. You didn't ask her to do it: you didn't even have an opportunity of preventing her doing it. Once the die was cast – and it was cast before you even came on the scene – nothing could be done. You must surely see that at this late stage it's quite impossible for me to do what you ask.' Her voice became vehemently persuasive and her neat side curls trembled ever so slightly as she drummed the table with her forefinger. 'Don't you see that I'm in the same position as Caesar's wife: you mustn't drag me into this. You don't seem to realize that the wife of a High Court judge is a person of position who must be beyond reproach in her personal life.' She paused and with a note of bitterness in her tone, went on, 'You seem crazily bent on ruining yourself and involving me at the same time – and all for no reason. You've already made things more difficult for me by going to Gethin without my knowledge. That wasn't a very fair thing to do.'

'I had to.'

'And now you want to destroy my life as well.'

'Helen, dear, I wish you'd try and see it my way. If you'll do what I ask, I'll take all the blame. I'll tell the world that the whole hideous mess is my fault, that you wanted to come forward before but that I wouldn't let you. I'll say anything you want to avoid, or at least minimize, the scandal you're so worried about.' He searched her face for some sign of encouragement but found none. 'I've considered this from every angle and reached the inescapable conclusion that only your word can save Celia.'

'And if I still refuse?'

'We've already discussed the alternative', he said quietly.

'You'll denounce me', said Helen thoughtfully. She drained her glass and started to pull on her gloves. 'Are you giving me a lift home?'

'Of course, my dear, and then I must go back and prepare a good opening speech for Gethin tomorrow. Incidentally are you coming to the free Luce show?'

'I'm not sure yet.'

They left the bar and walked to Christopher's Bentley which was parked in a near-by square. As they got in, Helen said:

'Ought you to drive with your hand like that?'

'It's much better now and I don't think it matters taking it out of the sling. As long as I don't have to exert any pressure on my thumb I can manage quite comfortably. Luckily this car has the old-fashioned right-hand gear change. The chief curse is that it's put paid to my week-end golf.'

He settled himself behind the wheel and pressed the starter button and a moment later they were gliding westwards. He dropped Helen at her home in Knightsbridge and continued on to his own without a further stop.

As he entered the hall, he heard voices in the drawing-room. He opened the door and went in. Celia and Robin were sitting together on the sofa and Marcus King-Selman sat opposite them.

'A council of war?' he asked with a faint smile as he closed the door behind him. Marcus immediately sprang to his feet.

'I'd better be going', he said, addressing himself to Celia and ignoring Christopher.

'Not on my account, please', Christopher said. 'I shall be going to my study to work in a moment.' He stooped and kissed his wife on top of her head. 'How are you, sweetheart? Hullo, where's Robin disappeared to?' The distant sound of the laboratory door slamming gave him his answer. He made throat-clearing noises and took a new tube of cough capsules from his pocket. He threw them on to his wife's lap. 'Open them for me, sweetheart, while I get a drink.'

'Where did you buy these?' she asked after a pause as she struggled to remove the plastic tape round the cap.

'I got them on the way back just now. Why?'

'I just wondered', Celia replied. 'Here, you have a go', she added, passing the tube to Marcus. 'I don't want to break my nails.'

Christopher turned round from the cocktail cabinet.

'Here's luck', he said.

Marcus glared at him. 'I think your conduct towards

Celia has been quite despicable', he said, suddenly bursting forth. 'I wouldn't have believed that an Englishman could behave so contemptibly. No, don't try and stop me, Celia', he said as she put out a vaguely restraining hand. 'I've been wanting to express myself for a very long time. You first of all steal my wife and, not content to do that, you then treat her as I wouldn't stoop to treat the lowest native in my employ. If the law didn't take a hidebound view of such things, I'd give you the thrashing you so richly deserve – and enjoy doing it as well.' Christopher, drink in hand, his eyes bright, alert and faintly mocking, stood watching Marcus in silence. He made no effort to cut short the tirade and Marcus continued, 'Let me tell you this, Henham, if you don't put matters straight with the police before midday tomorrow, you'll have to reckon with me. I'll give you till then and no longer.'

A deep silence followed and then Christopher said suavely:

'I had been about, before you spoke, to thank you for having given Celia so much of your time these last two weeks. I know she has enjoyed seeing you again and that you have helped to distract her mind from the matter which has been worrying both of us and about which I know she has told you. In fact you couldn't have come on leave at a more propitious moment, my dear fellow.' His tone hardened perceptibly as he went on, 'But perhaps from now on you would kindly stay away from my house and from my wife and seek your pleasures elsewhere. And you might let me have that tube of capsules before you completely crush it in your grip.'

Without looking at his hand, Marcus threw the tube at him. He caught it neatly in his good hand and put it in his pocket. Marcus meanwhile continued to stand in the middle of the room looking rather like a grand opera baritone after an exhausting aria and Christopher took out the capsules, tipped one into the palm of his hand and dexterously tossed it back into his mouth, at the same moment swallowing. It was a well-practised action and Marcus, whose outburst had given way to baleful taciturnity, watched him with absorbed interest. A moment later he stalked out of the room.

CHAPTER NINE

CHRISTOPHER HENHAM bent his knees in order to be able to see his face in the robing-room mirror. He was robed ready for court apart from his wig and this he always put on last after first carefully combing and brushing his hair. This was not the superfluous action it might seem to be as he had long discovered that if he clamped his wig on to ruffled hair, the sight when it was removed several hours later was of a shipwrecked mariner emerging from an oily sea.

He adjusted his wig with care, took a final look at himself in the mirror to straighten his bands and left the robing-room. On arrival in the corridor in the vicinity of Mr. Justice Riley's court he found a scene reminiscent of the Stock Exchange just after a prince of finance has hurled himself off Beachy Head. He managed to cleave a way through the crowd and eventually reached the door where the hapless attendant on duty was perspiring freely from the undue exertion of trying to keep the throng at bay. He grunted as he let Christopher in and quickly cut off two women who tried to sweep through in his wake.

Inside, the scene was more orderly, though every available seat was filled and the gangways were half-choked with standing spectators who had managed to get in under one false colour or another. Two of Godfrey Luce's more elderly and devoted fans had, thanks to the tenebrous atmosphere of the corridor outside, passed through by murmuring 'Bar student' in confident tones. Once in the court they had produced small collapsible camp-stools and settled down comfortably. An indulgent usher chose not to notice them.

Alfred Exley, who had arrived in court in advance of Christopher, had arranged his papers for him and placed a carafe of water near-by. This was one of the moments that Christopher always revelled in, when, recognized by everyone present, he would give a superb preliminary display of quintessential urbanity and self-assurance. Slowly and with every movement accented he took a tube of cough capsules from his pocket and shook the last three on to the desk in front of him – he had had a bad night and realized with a frown that he had consumed more than he had imagined. He knew that his foible was being observed and commented on by the avidly-watching spectators as he laid one of the capsules on to his extended tongue and washed it down with water from the carafe. His whole performance was much more like Godfrey Luce playing the part of a Q.C. in a film. He looked round at the benches behind him, smiled at Celia and studiously ignored Marcus, who was sitting beside her. While he basked, he received and dispatched with unruffled calm last-minute messages via the acolytes who swanned about him.

He gazed up at the high walls of the courtroom and reflected, not for the first time, on their resemblance to scenes of the Baron's Castle in a more pretentious production of *Cinderella*. The noise around him of unsuppressed conversation was like that of a swarm of bluebottles round a fishmonger's barrow on a hot day in August. It suddenly died away and everyone stood up as an usher opened the door behind the judge's seat and called out 'Silence please'.

Mr. Justice Riley entered, nodded perfunctorily in acknowledgement of counsel's courtly bows and settled himself in his seat after the manner of a hen squatting on a hot dust patch. A few moments later Christopher Henham rose to his feet.

'May it please your lordship, I am instructed in this case, together with my learned friend Mr. Tuft, on behalf of the petitioner, Mr. Godfrey Luce, who prays for the dissolution of his marriage on the grounds of the respondent's adultery with the co-respondent, a young artist named Rafael Rink. My learned friends Mr. Quirkly and Mr. Bond appear on behalf of the respondent, Lady Jane Luce, and my learned friend, Mr. Samson, represents the co-respondent. My lord, the case —.'

'Mr. Henham, one moment please', interrupted the judge. 'There's a person at the back of the public gallery with a cough like the bark of a sea-lion. Would she be kind enough either to leave or else control the noise. Coughing is usually only a matter of self-control', he added, looking at Christopher. 'Yes, go on, Mr. Henham.'

'As I was about to say to your lordship, it is very much to be regretted that this case comes to be defended and that the respondent has seen fit, since proceedings were first commenced, to hurl abuse and utterly unjustifiable accusations at my client. The petitioner's case is quite simply this: that on three occasions in July of last year, the respondent and the co-respondent cohabited together at a bungalow on the south coast . . .'

As Christopher continued his long and lucid opening address, which was interrupted only by two brief spasms of coughing which he quickly subdued, Marcus turned to Celia.

'Why does she bother to defend the case?' he whispered.

'It's obvious', Celia hissed back. 'She mayn't have much use for her husband as a bed companion but she

72

doesn't want to be thrown out of his house without a bean. She hasn't any money of her own and young Rafael Rink has less. One can't exactly see an Earl's daughter who has been married to wealth for some years enthusiastically embracing domestic life with an indigent artist. It's only natural she should want to go on having the best of both worlds.'

'Why were you so keen on coming to-day?' Marcus asked suddenly.

'Because I knew that you wanted to.' He shot her a quick look and was about to say something further when he caught the admonishing eye of one of the ushers and returned his attention to Christopher.

It was Christopher's experience that reading aloud was much more liable to provoke his cough than ordinary speaking. Unfortunately the time came in his opening speech when he had to refer to a voluminous bundle of correspondence and read acrimonious extracts to the court. Before starting on this, he quickly swallowed another capsule, but by the time he was nearing the end he was having obvious difficulty in suppressing his accursed affliction.

When the lunch adjournment was reached, he had completed his opening speech and had examined Godfrey Luce in chief. The first few questions of cross-examination had already been fired at the great man and these gave every promise of providing an afternoon of high-voltage entertainment. It was with considerable difficulty that the public seats were cleared and in fact the two Luce fans on camp-stools protested energetically on being ejected in the middle of the picnic lunch which they had thoughtfully brought with them.

Christopher was about to leave the court when his opponent, Mr. Quirkly, spoke to him.

'I say, Henham, my clerk has just reminded me of

something I've got to do at two o'clock. I wonder if we could go and see the judge and ask him not to sit till a quarter past. Would you object?'

'No, that's all right as far as I'm concerned, but do you want me to come with you?'

'If you don't mind. I never like seeing the judge alone in the middle of a case. I think, for appearance's sake, it would be better if we both went.'

'As you wish.' Christopher stood hesitant for a moment and then, suddenly espying Robin standing by one of the doors, he beckoned to him. Robin turned and spoke to Celia who was just leaving the court with Marcus and then came across to his stepfather. He was scowling and at that moment looked a spoilt and disagreeable young man.

'Do me a favour, would you, Robin?' said Christopher. 'Slip down to my Chambers and tell Alfred or Maureen or whoever is in the clerks' office to phone the solicitors in the Becker case to say that the consultation fixed for this evening must be postponed. Also ask someone to get me some more cough capsules and bring them to court after lunch. O.K.?'

Robin nodded, after an ostentatious pause to make up his mind whether or not to comply with his stepfather's request.

Christopher and Mr. Quirkly approached Mr. Justice Riley's private room and the latter knocked.

'I'm so sorry to bother you, judge', he began and then said, 'Oh good morning, Lady Riley, I didn't see you in court.'

'I wasn't there', replied Helen. 'I've only just arrived and come straight to my husband's room.' She had a strained look about her but gave Christopher a taut little smile as she turned toward him. 'I heard you coughing away as I came past the back of the court so knew the case was in full swing.'

Gethin Riley had been silently disrobing himself during this exchange but now, buttoning up his waistcoat, he turned to face the two advocates.

'At least when a member of the public distracts one with persistent coughing, one can order him or her to be removed, but when it's an advocate the hapless judge seems to have no remedy. Eh, Quirkly?'

Mr. Quirkly dutifully laughed and looked at Christopher.

'Why don't you try one of Gethin's Umujubes?' asked Helen. 'Something new might do the trick.'

'My coughing hasn't been unusually tiresome this morning, has it?'

'It's always tiresome', said the judge. 'The trouble is that you've become immunized against the effect of those capsules you take. You either ought to increase the dose, as every drug addict has to, or else try something different as Helen suggests.' As he spoke he took a tin from his pocket and shook three or four lozenges into an envelope. 'Here, take these this afternoon and Quirkly and I may be able to hear ourselves think for a change.'

At ten minutes past two everyone was back in their place waiting for the judge to enter when Maureen hurried up to Christopher and handed him the fresh tube of cough capsules which he had asked for. She avoided looking at him and was about to rush away again when he asked her to undo them and roll two or three out on to the desk. She did this as though it were a thoroughly distasteful task and impatiently shook three small golden capsules out to join the single one left over from the morning. Then without a word she flew from the court just as Riley, J., made his entry.

The cross-examination of Godfrey Luce by Mr. Quirkly continued. It was long and somewhat repetitious, but elicited a number of fascinating details of the Luces' domestic life which exhilarated the public. On a number of occasions, Christopher rose to object to certain questions, but on most of them was summarily squashed by the judge, who always added insult to injury by looking round the court for the silent approbation of everyone present. Christopher's final intervention in the cross-examination was prefaced by a throaty outburst which temporarily deprived him of speech. As it subsided, Mr. Justice Riley smiled at him without love or affection.

'Take one of those *other* lozenges, Mr. Henham. Go on, take one now and then perhaps you will be able to get through a sentence without interrupting yourself.'

Christopher said nothing, being only too well aware that in court Gethin Riley had the whip hand. He picked up the envelope which contained the Umujubes. The judge watched every movement and not until he saw Christopher take his hand away from his mouth did he speak.

'Yes, Mr. Henham, I believe that you were about to object to Mr. Quirkly's last question. Let me say that I can see nothing wrong with it, but of course I will listen to any remarks you may wish to address to me on the subject.'

There was silence as he waited for Christopher to reply, but the latter appeared just to stand there and say nothing. Suddenly a stream of words exploded from him only to trail away unintelligibly. His face was seized in spasmic contortions and a moment later his whole body crumpled and slumped across the desk. For one awful long split second he lay grotesquely still with his wig askew over one ear, and then before everyone's horrified gaze his body writhed in three violent convulsions and finally lay still for ever.

CHAPTER TEN

ALMOST inevitably Detective-Superintendent Manton burnt the tip of his tongue on the scalding canteen tea. He flinched, jerked the cup away from his lips and in so doing spilt some of the contents on to the table where it coalesced with two large isolated pools of the same tasteless and odourless fluid.

Around him police officers of every rank and size were busily engaged in efforts to satisfy their inner men, and prodigious mounds of eggs and chips were being demolished and washed down into large capacious stomachs. The young P.C. opposite Manton wiped the crumbs of his third rock bun from his chin and with a small detached belch undid another button of his tunic before tackling the fourth.

Manton, however, was oblivious of his surroundings and his brow was furrowed in deep concentration as he blew and sipped his tea. It was a problem which had been exercising his mind on and off for a whole week and one which was still unresolved.

'You're wanted on the phone, Mr. Manton.' He looked up and saw one of the canteen servers waving the instrument at him from the far side of the room. With a sigh he got up and weaved his way across the crowded floor, pushing once more into the background of his mind the problem of whether to re-do the bathroom in dove grey and mushroom pink or Atlantic green and foam white. Somehow it would have to be settled by the week-end as he and Marjorie were reckoning to buy the paint and start on the job then.

'Superintendent Manton here', he said, taking the receiver from the girl.

'Oh, thank heavens I've found you', said a calm but plainly relieved voice. 'Will you come to the Commissioner's office straight away please?'

The total unexpectedness of the summons coupled with the knowledge that practical jokes are not unknown at the Yard caused Manton to proceed with caution.

'Who is it speaking?' he asked politely.

'Miss Gaffney, the Commissioner's secretary', she said, and added crisply, 'Now will you please come at once as everyone's waiting.'

Mystified but hoping for the best Manton hurried along the labyrinthine corridors and eventually arrived outside the Commissioner's office. He paused a moment to straighten his tie and pat his hair down and then knocked. Inside were the Commissioner, Deputy Commissioner and Assistant Commissioner (Crime) who was Manton's own departmental chief.

'Come in and sit down', said the Commissioner briskly. The three men watched him as he walked across the room and the A.C.C. gave him a reassuring wink. 'Ever heard of a Q.C. called Henham?' asked the Commissioner as soon as Manton was seated.

'Yes, sir. In fact I know him slightly.'

'You do, eh?' The Commissioner gave the assembled company a pleased look as though all credit for the acquaintanceship was his. 'He wasn't a close friend of yours, I hope?'

The tense was not lost on Manton. 'No, sir. But is he dead?'

The Commissioner nodded. 'Yes; this afternoon; in rather curious circumstances. Here are the facts such as we know them.' When he finally finished speaking, he fixed Manton with his famous fishlike stare and said, 'Not an easy one, eh, Manton? Will require considerable tact and much discretion. Sort of job wrongly handled could cause a few heads to roll. Mine; yours.' He stopped suddenly and intensified his stare so that Manton felt he was expected to say something.

'And you want me to undertake this inquiry, sir?'

'Of course. Why else should I have told you all this? Why else should these other two important gentlemen have been here but to hear me brief you? Your Assistant Commissioner considers that you're the man for the job and I agree with him.' He surveyed his senior lieutenants once more. 'All right, gentlemen? Good, then we won't waste further time as Superintendent Manton will want to start his inquiries without delay. By the way, Manton,' he added, as they were making for the door, 'don't forget that I'm just as keen to keep my head on my shoulders as I'm sure you are yours.'

'No, sir, I'll remember all you've said about decapitation', Manton replied, and beneath his breath added, 'Even if it does mean disappointing the crowds.'

In murder cases involving a husband or wife – and from what Manton had been told this gave every indication of being a case of murder – it is almost a police axiom that the first suspect is the surviving spouse and initial efforts are always directed to eliminate, or incriminate, him or her. It follows, of course, that murders of bachelors and spinsters present a more subtle problem and usually require a more flexible approach in the early stages of their investigation.

Accordingly, at ten past five the same afternoon Manton stood once more on the Henhams' doorstep in Kensington. The moon-faced Doris let him in and told him that Mrs. Henham was resting in her bedroom. On the way to the drawing-room, she suddenly said, 'Mr. King-Selman has only just left her and the doctor's been and given her some tablets. You see, the master's death gave her quite a shock.' Manton didn't really believe that Celia's reaction to her husband's death had been quite so lukewarm as Doris made it sound, though it was evident that Doris herself was not unduly bothered by the event. She went on, 'Anyway I'll go and tell her you're here. Just make yourself comfortable.' A minute or two later she poked her head round the door again. 'She's coming down. I must say I didn't think she'd see you.' She hovered uncertainly for a moment and then added hopefully, 'I must get back to my comp.'

'Comp.?'

'That's right. Don't you do comps.? No, I suppose you wouldn't have the time. Oh, but this one's real lovely. It's a lingerie comp. and you have to choose the piece you think would most suit Marilyn Monroe. They're all in different colours and the winner gets a free trip to Paris and a pressure cooker.'

'Sounds simply terrific', replied Manton encouragingly, at the same time wondering whether Doris herself made any use of some of the more utilitarian female foundation garments.

'I hear the mistress coming now', said Doris, and disappeared with the fascinating rapidity of the Cheshire cat.

The first thing that Manton noticed about Celia was that she had obviously been crying. Her eyes were red and her complexion was congested despite efforts to conceal the ravages of her tears. She was dressed in a plain black frock whose only relief was white piping round the collar, cuffs and hemline.

'I'm very sorry to have to trouble you at a time like

80

this, Mrs. Henham, but I would be grateful if you could spare me a few minutes.'

'Yes, I quite understand that you've got your job to do, Inspector. Doris did tell me your name but I'm afraid I've already forgotten it.'

'Manton. I'm a Detective-Superintendent at the Yard.'

'Yes, of course.' She wiped a hand across her forehead and sat down on the edge of the sofa, at the same time reaching for a cigarette. Manton lit it for her and sat down in the opposite chair. He was about to ask her a first formal question when she spoke.

'I suppose you have no doubt that my husband was murdered?'

'There's no evidence of that at the moment, Mrs. Henham', he replied carefully.

'Maybe not evidence, but when someone suddenly drops dead, poisoned, it's usually murder, isn't it?'

'We shall know more about that when we have the result of the post-mortem examination.'

Celia shuddered and her hand trembled violently as she lifted the cigarette to her lips. Manton noticed this and also stored away in his mind for future recollection her assumption of murder by poison. A quarter of an hour later under Manton's expert guidance she had related to him many varied details of her recent life; of her previous marriage and its dissolution; of her second marriage to Christopher Henham two and a half years ago.

'Was Mr. Henham cited as co-respondent in your divorce action?' Manton interrupted her to ask.

'How could he be? It would have wrecked his career. No, Marcus gave me a divorce. But we've always re-mained good friends.' Manton winced at the well-worn and usually meaningless expression, but Celia now seemed to want to talk and he was content to let her prattle on. All the while he noticed, however, that the one topic she studiously avoided was that of her recent motor accident and forthcoming trial. Eventually he gently introduced the subject himself.

'Yes, I suppose you read about it in the papers', said Celia, looking away from him. 'Presumably British police being allegedly like the mills of God, I shall still stand my trial for manslaughter even though my husband has just been murdered.'

There she goes again, Manton thought. She at any rate hasn't the slightest doubt that he was murdered – or at least pretends not to have. Aloud he said:

'How did your husband react to your motor accident?'

'He was naturally very upset about it – terribly upset and worried in fact.' She paused and her lips trembled. 'I don't think I can go on talking about him. It's all so awful. He was the most precious possession I've ever had and now – now I have lost him for ever.' She buried her face in her hands and silently sobbed. Manton, who spent much of his life interviewing people under the stress of strong emotions, waited for a moment or two. Though he was not infrequently filled with sympathy and compassion on such occasions, he had never yet allowed sentiment to sway his judgment. At last Celia looked across at him.

'Is that all, Superintendent?'

'Not really, Mrs. Henham', he said with a sympathetic smile. 'There are one or two further matters I'd like to ask you about if you feel up to it.'

'Very well, I might as well get it all over in one.'

Manton forbore to point out that this was a quite unfounded hope and went on, 'Supposing for one moment that your husband did die as a result of swallowing poison, it would seem probable that it was administered by means of one of his cough sweets. I gather he used to take

Capstick's Cough Capsules for his throat. Can you help me at all about his supply of them?'

'But of course it wasn't one of his own capsules that was poisoned', said Celia vehemently. 'It was one that Gethin Riley had given him.' Seeing Manton's expression she continued, 'Oh, I know you think I'm crazy to suggest that a High Court judge hands poisoned cough lozenges around, but that's precisely what happened – and anyway you don't know him. He hated Christopher. Well, now I've said it, but you wanted the truth.'

'Look, Mrs. Henham, I know you're suggesting that Mr. Justice Riley deliberately poisoned your husband, but can you give me any possible motive for his doing such a thing?'

For a moment Celia was thoughtfully silent. At length she said, 'He has always loathed Christopher and been madly jealous of him. I've sometimes felt that it was almost a pathological condition. He's certainly the last man on earth you'd ever want to fall foul of. Christopher and he had known each other since they were Bar students and . . .' Her voice trailed away with the sentence leading nowhere.

'Was this hatred reciprocated by your husband?'

'Christopher couldn't hate anyone. He just refused to let Gethin Riley upset him and that seemed to annoy the judge more than ever, which shows you the sort of man he is. He's the type to harbour a grudge from decade to decade.'

'Do you know of any particular grudge he harboured against your husband?'

'No', said Celia with too obvious reluctance. 'But Christopher was always a bit evasive about his relations with Gethin and I often felt that there were aspects of it about which he never wanted to speak.'

'I see', said Manton in his most judicial and non-committal tone, and after a pause added, 'Is there anything else you wish to tell me, Mrs. Henham?'

There was not and a few minutes later he was on his way back to the Yard. He decided that there were three matters to ponder over. First there was Celia's conviction that her husband had been murdered by a High Court judge. Next there was her failure to suggest in any way that she had not been driving her car at the time of the fatal accident. And finally there was her apparent ignorance of her husband's approach to Manton a few days before his death.

Of the three, the last two seemed to Manton to be the more significant.

On arrival at Scotland Yard, Manton went straight to the Assistant Commissioner's room. He felt that his interview with Celia Henham hardly called for a direct report to the Commissioner and in any event this direct-reporting-to-the-boss business was, in his view, deceptively simple. It sounded fine, but was a practice which was sprung with hidden traps – man-traps, too.

'So now you want to go and see Mr. Justice Riley?' said the A.C.C. when Manton had finished speaking.

'I think I ought to go and see him next, sir, for two reasons. In the first place he was an eyewitness of Henham's death and secondly there's the business of the cough lozenges to be explained.'

'Also he'll probably be extremely huffy if you don't call on him soon. You know what *prima donna* temperaments some judges have and Riley, J. certainly seems to be one of them. But you'll have to tread warily so far as the cough sweets are concerned. Don't forget that at the moment we've got no evidence that Henham died of poison. "Evidence" being the operative word.'

Manton nodded. 'Perhaps I might use your phone, sir,

and see if Dr. Dill can give me any news. Where was he doing the P.M.?"

'Holborn public mortuary. Sturdy is there and I thought it would also be a good thing if Talper attended. Although he's now out at a division, he has a prospective interest in the case and I knew you'd be glad to have him working with you.'

'Couldn't suit me better, sir.' Manton lifted the receiver and asked for the mortuary. The A.C.C. closed the file he had been glancing at and with a sigh tossed it jauntily into his out-tray.

'A thirty-six-page letter from Miss Hispano-Belle', he said conversationally.

'Thirty-six pages?' echoed Manton.

'Yes, one of her shorter ones.'

'Who is the lady, sir?'

'Miss Hispano-Belle? She lives in Notting Hill and writes letters. She may also eat and sleep, though she can't have much time left for either. Her present complaint concerns the Foreign Secretary. It appears that he persists in sending her importunate invitations to lunch. She receives them regularly at ten past eleven every morning.'

'By special messenger, I presume?'

'No. By telepathy.'

Manton laughed. 'Do you have to answer her letters, sir?'

'I used to acknowledge them, but that only roused her to greater epistolary efforts; so now I don't. In any event she finishes this one by saying that she is sending copies of it to Mao-tse-Tung, the Queen of Tonga and Gilbert Harding and I'm sure one of them will leap to reply.'

The phone rang and Manton answered it.

'Is Detective-Chief Inspector Sturdy there . . .? Hullo, Inspector. Superintendent Manton here. I'm speaking from the Assistant Commissioner's room. Has Dr. Dill got any line on the cause of death yet?'

'Here, let me have that earphone', said the A.C.C. unhooking it from the back of the apparatus.

Detective-Inspector Sturdy's voice came down the line, articulate and without emotion. He might have been reporting on the dimensions of the mortuary rather than on the suddenly deceased body within it.

'The doctor has no doubt that poison was the cause of death, but he says he can't say how it was administered without a detailed lab. analysis of the stomach contents and other organs. We're getting them bottled and I'll bring them along as soon as he's finished, sir.'

'Any views on the size of the dose?'

'Hold on, sir, I'll go and have a word with him.' There was a pause and then his voice came through again. 'He says it must have been a plenty strong one. Whoever it was didn't mean to leave anything to chance.'

'O.K. Thanks, Inspector. You might tell Dr. Dill that I'll be getting in touch with him shortly.'

'And now,' said the A.C.C., 'off you go and tackle the judge. But for heaven's sake handle him as you would a volcano scheduled for early eruption; and if I'm not still here when you're through, get in touch with me at home.'

Manton found the Rileys' house in a secluded street not far from Harrods. It was the middle one in a short Georgian terrace, whose façade, though neat and comely, gave small hint of the comfort and luxurious amenities which lay behind.

The door was opened by a female servant who might have stepped out of one of the early scenes in Noel Coward's *Cavalcade*. Manton felt quite certain that she was habitually addressed by her surname and was fascinated by her gait, though this hardly seemed an apposite word to describe the movement of one who was unquestionably mounted on castors.

After leaving him to stand alone in the hall for a short time, she glided back to his side and ushered him into the study. This looked over the tiny back garden and Manton was gazing out of the window at coloured tubs and reflecting how much brighter they looked than the droopy plants they held, when the door opened and Mr. Justice Riley came in.

Manton, of course, knew most of the judges of the Queen's Bench Division, whose whims and caprices he and his colleagues had to try and keep abreast of, but those of the Chancery and Probate, Divorce and Admiralty Divisions of the High Court were only names to him and often not even that. Sir Gethin Riley, however, had made certain by his conduct that his name was known to the maximum public, and Manton could well understand this, as the judge without a word went and sat down behind his desk and then fixed him with a cold unfriendly stare. His failure to offer any greeting or invite his visitor to be seated could not have been more markedly deliberate. There passed through Manton's mind the saying that small men frequently suffer from inferiority complexes on account of their size, but he imagined not even all the psychiatrists in the square mile north of Oxford Street could catalogue all their numerous and varied manifestations. In the case of Mr. Justice Riley, however, the attempt was to offset his five feet four inches by all the worst vices begotten of a life spent in the law. Pomposity and sarcasm were blended with a pontifical disdain of his fellow-creatures and led to all his conversation being conducted like a cross-examination of a palpably dishonest and unpleasant witness.

'I hope I haven't called at a very inconvenient time, my lord', Manton said, and paused for the judge to reply.

'I had rather expected that the Commissioner would give me a ring', replied the judge frigidly. 'I certainly had not anticipated the unheralded arrival of a policeman on my doorstep. Quite obviously things are done differently at the Yard nowadays. However, since you are here, you had better state your business.' He had spoken in quiet, measured tones without ever shifting his gaze from Manton's face.

'I've come to see you, my lord, about the death of Mr. Henham in your court this afternoon.'

'Yes; but we are not in court now, officer.'

'No, my lord', replied Manton, wondering hard what might be the import of this observation.

'Then kindly stop calling me "my lord". I am not a peer of the realm. "Sir" will be sufficient.'

The eyes of the two men met, like those of snake and mongoose taking up positions to spar to the death.

'May I ask you some questions, sir?'

'You may, I suppose, ask them, but I do not propose to answer.' Again the judge paused to observe the effect of his goading remarks on Manton—at least that was how it appeared to Manton himself.

'Am I to inform the Commissioner, sir, that you do not wish to be interviewed about this afternoon's events?' he asked.

Mr. Justice Riley compressed his thin lips and pouted them out. He then opened the leather blotter on his desk and picked up a sheet of quarto paper which Manton could see bore the stamp of the Royal Courts of Justice at the top.

'I have already prepared a statement covering my knowledge of the affair and thus an interview is superfluous.' He paused and added, 'If the Commissioner had taken the trouble to phone me, I could have told him this and you could have been saved a journey and been more profitably employed catching burglars or whatever it is the senior officers of the Metropolitan police force do.' He slid the sheet of paper across the desk to Manton, who picked it up without evident enthusiasm. It read:

'To-day, Wednesday, 29th April, I started to try a defended divorce action in which Mr. Christopher Henham appeared as leading counsel for the petitioner. Mr. Henham was as usual bothered by a persistent throat cough and throughout the morning session was constantly consuming the cough capsules which he takes to alleviate that condition. About half an hour after the court had resumed following the luncheon adjournment, he became subject to an extremely severe bout of coughing which effectively held up the proceedings. I advised him to take a lozenge. He appeared to do so and almost immediately afterwards collapsed and died. I immediately gave instructions that the police were to be sent for and that no one was to leave the court. I then retired to my private room.' There followed the signature 'Gethin Riley' and beneath it the words 'A Justice of the High Court'.

Manton pondered this short and quite inadequate statement for a brief moment and then decided to grasp the nettle boldly.

'There are a number of questions I'd like to ask you on this statement, sir.'

'Why?'

'To amplify one or two points and to clear up some ambiguities.'

'Ambiguities?'

The judge's expression and tone indicated that he had been jabbed in a sensitive spot and Manton found his reaction most satisfactory.

'In the first place, sir, I'd like to go into rather more

89

detail about these cough lozenges. I gather that you gave Mr. Henham some of yours when he visited you in your room during the lunch adjournment.'

'That is so.'

Manton was taken aback by this equable agreement and realized at once that it led him on to distinctly treacherous ground.

'It has been suggested, sir, that it was one of your lozenges that Mr. Henham took immediately prior to his death.'

'How should I know such a thing? Do you suppose he held it up for my inspection before putting it into his mouth?' It was at this point that the telephone suddenly rang. Before Mr. Justice Riley could lift the receiver, however, the ringing ceased and Manton guessed that somewhere in the house someone was answering it on an extension. Nevertheless the judge put the receiver to his ear and listened in rather sinister silence for some moments before replacing it. When he did so, Manton answered the interrupted question.

'No, sir, but it has been suggested that you in fact exhorted him to take one of the lozenges which you had given him.'

The silence which greeted this observation was the same which might surround two armed enemies playing a game of mortal hide-and-seek in the dark.

'And are you suggesting that the statement which I have just given you is not the truth?'

'Not at all, sir; but it doesn't mention that particular point.'

'Tell me,' said the judge softly, 'has the cause of Henham's death yet been ascertained?'

'He died of poison, sir.'

'There are many poisons. Which one?'

Manton's inclination was to tell him to mind his own

business, but with reluctance he said, 'Probably potassium cyanide.'

'I see. And what is your evidence as to the manner in which it was administered?'

'It seems a distinct possibility that —' The sentence was cut off by the judge's curt interjection.

'And do possibilities pass for evidence in the criminal courts these days?'

'It may be some time before —' Again Manton was not allowed to complete his sentence.

'Perhaps next time – if such there be – that you or one of your colleagues come to see me, you would be so good as to base your questions on established facts – on evidence – and not on a heap of hypothetical supposition. That may be the way in which you conduct your interviews with those who are less able to look after themselves, but *I* have no intention of supplying you with a pond for a general fishing expedition and I shall not think twice about reporting to the Home Secretary any repetition of such methods.'

The door opened and Manton turned to see the parlour-maid who had let him in standing there.

'Hislop, kindly show this person to the door', said Mr. Justice Riley in his unfriendliest tone.

A few yards down the street, Manton entered a public call box. He felt that the interview had been a novel experience and far from a waste of time.

'Manton here, sir', he said when he heard the A.C.C.'s voice at the other end of the line. 'I'd like to come and see you straight away.'

'Right, I'm at home and will expect you. Know who did it yet?'

'I know who I hope did it, sir', he replied with a glance back toward the Rileys' house.

·   ·   ·   ·   ·

Detective-Superintendent Simon Manton and Detective-Sergeant Andrew Talper sat together in Manton's office, which was roughly the size of a large tea-chest. Big Ben had just struck eight o'clock and the corridors of Scotland Yard were relatively free and peaceful. From time to time an officer on late duty journeyed whistling from one part of the large building to another.

Manton had only recently attained the prime age of the forties and was one of the youngest Detective-Superintendents in the force. He was one of the successful products of the Trenchard College system and had been promoted to his present rank on merit in advance of a flood-tide which suddenly made it as common as that of Colonel in a South American revolutionary army.

He was a person of thoroughly pleasant appearance whose most distinguishing feature was his large and highly expressive bright blue eyes. Recently he had been disturbed by the speed with which his hair was leaving him, though Marjorie, his wife, had cheerfully said she didn't mind his going discreetly thin in front, but on no account would she tolerate one of those bald patches of ever-increasing circumference on the crown of his head.

Talper at six feet topped Manton by three inches. He was broad-shouldered and as strong as the proverbial ox and his placid face was surmounted by thick dark curly hair. Manton and he had worked as a team on a number of murder cases, including a recent one in the West of England where they were sent in answer to a call for aid from the local Chief Constable. As a result of their successful solving of this case they had earned his fulsome praise for their work.

Manton listened quietly as Talper reported on the autopsy which Dr. Dill had completed about an hour before

'Even before he started carving him up, he had a pretty good idea that it was potassium cyanide poisoning. There were pinkish patches over his back, chest and stomach and as for his face, it was just like a rather anæmic radish.'

'This is the first case I've had of poisoning by potassium cyanide,' said Manton, 'but isn't it our old friend bitter almonds – the odour that used so to entrance the writers of crime fiction before the war? Phials of the stuff used to be a standard issue to all their villains in those days. Dose when cornered, one toothful.'

'That's it, sir, and you could smell it plain as anything when he opened the stomach and chest. Just like a Japanese flower garden it was.'

Manton privately took leave to doubt the aptitude of Sergeant Talper's simile and said:

'So far so good, but we're stymied until the lab. has analysed all the bits and pieces Dr. Dill bottled and can tell us the size of the dose and the probable means of administration. And that may take some time.'

'Surely it can only have been via a cough lozenge, sir?'

'Seems that way. But which cough lozenge? One of his own – or one the judge gave him?'

'The judge's are called "Umujubes" – bit of a surprise to me that, sir. I'd always imagined they sucked liquorice allsorts on the Bench. The deceased's were Capstick's Cough Capsules. Incidentally I've taken specimens of each to the lab.'

'A capsule would presumably be a far better carrier of poison than a Umujube, which is, after all, a sucker.'

'I had a word with Dr. Dill about that, sir. He reckoned it would take three or four minutes for a capsule to melt in the stomach and release its contents.'

'And what do we know in this case?'

'That it was not more than a minute after putting the thing into his mouth that he collapsed. We've had statements from everyone who was in court at the time and one minute is the very outside estimate given. Some say it was

93

almost as soon as he took his hand away from his mouth that he showed signs of something being wrong.'

'Which rules out a capsule?'

'Seems to.'

'And leaves a Umujube.' There was a thoughtful silence and Manton then added, almost as a postscript, 'And of course there are several witnesses, including eminent lawyers and court officials, who say quite definitely that the judge was exhorting Henham to take a Umujube and not a capsule.'

'Which rather excludes the judge as a murderer,' said Talper complacently, 'since he would hardly have palmed him off a poisoned Umujube and then have told him before a whole cloud of witnesses to suck the thing until he be dead.'

'Mmm. It requires a lot of careful thought', Manton said slowly. 'I agree that it seems unlikely on the face of it, but it could be that the judge was an innocent agent in the disposal of the poisoned lozenge.'

'How could that be?'

'I've no idea, but it's a possibility to be explored. Tell me, Andy,' he said, changing the subject abruptly, 'how many capsules and Umujubes were found on the deceased or in his vicinity?'

'On the desk in front of him was an envelope containing two Umujubes and a third one was found on the floor beneath his seat. As regards the capsules, there were two lying on the desk and in his trouser pocket was a tube with four missing. I've made inquiries and I understand that it was his habit to shake three or four out on to the desk so that they were handy and he didn't have to fiddle about with the tube every time he wanted one.'

'I see', said Manton. 'So if there were four missing from the tube in his pocket and you only found two on the desk, it means there are two unaccounted for – presumably swallowed and one of them very possibly a poisoned one. Has anyone checked on when and where he purchased his last supply?'

'I haven't done so yet, sir.'

'We must find that out. Incidentally, what sort of container is this "tube" we keep on talking about?'

'It's made of light metal, is about four inches long, elliptical in shape and has a screw top.'

'How many capsules does it hold?'

'Ten. That is this particular size.'

'What's the normal dose?'

'About one every three hours, but I gather Mr. Henham used to take one every half-hour or so when he was in court and particularly bothered by his throat.'

'Quite an excessive dose. Aren't they dangerous in that quantity?'

'I don't think so, sir. The fact was he'd become immunized against their effect and had to keep on taking more and more.'

'Yes, presumably. Like Alice and the Red Queen.'

'Red Dean?' said Talper in surprise.

'No, queen. They were always having to run faster and faster to keep in the same place.'

'Oh', said Talper politely and waited for Manton to continue, which he did after a moment of thoughtful silence. 'Poison means long premeditation. And premeditation usually indicates a strong and unappeasable motive. At the moment we know nothing at all about motive. We must concentrate on it. Who needed to murder Christopher Henham, Q.C.? His wife? A High Court judge? or who? – and why?'

CHAPTER ELEVEN

'WHAT are you doing in here, Maureen?'
It was the following morning and Alfred Exley was standing in the doorway of Christopher Henham's room in Chambers. Maureen started guiltily and blushed under the clerk's calm but disapproving stare. She made a poor attempt at shutting a drawer of Christopher's desk without attracting attention and the clerk went on, 'And why have you opened that drawer?'

'I – er – I just thought I'd better . . .'

Alfred Exley cut short the stammering sentence. 'You have no right to be in here and even less to meddle with Mr. Henham's effects.'

The sternness of the rebuke made her blush even further but now her eyes flashed with anger.

'How dare you speak to me like that, treating me as if I were a prying stranger? Wasn't I Mr. Henham's secretary? Well, wasn't I?'

'No', said Alfred Exley quietly. 'No, you weren't. You're the Chambers' stenographer. Your services are not exclusive to any one member of the Chambers and they never have been, though you sometimes appear to have forgotten it.'

'I used to do all Mr. Henham's work, didn't I?' said Maureen, her tone still angry and consequently louder than necessary. 'He used to trust me to do all his confidential work for him, didn't he? I knew more about him than anyone else in Chambers.' Alfred Exley continued to stand in the doorway. His face was white and seemed to reflect complete revulsion at the whole distasteful scene. But Maureen, neither noticing nor caring, plunged on, 'Mr. Henham knew how to treat me. He didn't regard a girl in Chambers as just a typewriter. He had warm, human feelings. He appreciated me . . .'

'Stop it this instant, Maureen. You can't know what you're saying.' The clerk's voice cut her short with quiet authority. 'I think it would be better if you were to leave straight away. You may have your last few days off since you are so obviously in need of a rest. Your nerves are all on edge. I'll send you on your money and a testimonial.'

'Perhaps I might have a word with her before she goes', said Manton pleasantly. He had been standing unnoticed in the entrance hall for some moments and the clerk turned sharply at the sound of a strange voice. Manton introduced himself and continued, 'I'd also like to take a look round Mr. Henham's room, so perhaps I could combine matters and talk to Miss Fox at the same time.'

'Certainly, Superintendent', replied the clerk, coldly. He was not pleased at Manton's wish to speak to Maureen before having a word with him. It was rather akin to ignoring one's host at a party and his displeasure was increased by the arrogant look of triumph which Maureen unmistakably gave him. However, there seemed to be little he could do about the situation, other than stalk with dignity back across the hall to the office which he, the junior clerk and Maureen all shared. Manton closed the door of Christopher's room behind him and went over to the window where he perched himself comfortably on the broad sill.

'Do sit down, Miss Fox', he said conversationally, and when she had done so, went on, 'I gather you knew Mr. Henham very well.' She made no reply and he decided to be perfectly fair with her. 'You see, I couldn't help

97

overhearing what you said to the clerk just now. Would it be right to say that your relationship was a warmer and pleasanter one than the strict call of duty required?'

'Mr. Henham was always very good to me', she replied in an inexpressive monotone.

'I'm sure he was. Did he ever take you out?'

'Only twice. Each time was after we'd both been working here late and we were the only two left in Chambers.'

'Yes, very natural', Manton said soothingly. 'Where did you go? Dinner and a show – that sort of thing?'

'We just went out to dinner each time. We didn't want to go to a show.'

'Look, Miss Fox, it's clear to me that you're a sensible girl and that you probably know quite a bit about Mr. Henham which would help me in my inquiry into his death, so you don't mind my asking you some rather personal questions, do you? I'm afraid police officers have to be terribly inquisitive', he added with a smile. He watched her carefully as he spoke. He was sure that she could supply him with some interesting background material if so minded. Secretary girl-friends usually became the repositories of the most intimate, and often surprising, secrets. She didn't reply, but her manner indicated that she was waiting to hear his first question.

'Was Mr. Henham happily married?' he asked.

'Of course.'

'A lot of men aren't', he said dryly.

'I'm sure he was very fond of his wife in his own way.'

'Now, that's an interesting qualification', replied Manton encouragingly.

'Well, what I mean is, a lot of men like Mr. Henham are happily married but that isn't to say they never look at another woman.'

'Very true', he said in his most winning tone. 'From which I gather that Mr. Henham enjoyed female company in addition to that provided by his wife. Like many men he probably found that he required another's companionship to achieve complete fulfilment and to exploit his psyche.' Not for one brief moment did he believe such airy nonsense or even have much idea what it meant, if anything at all, but he could see that it was the right line on which to feed Maureen. As he spoke a faraway reflective look came into her eyes.

'Yes,' she said dreamily, 'he was just like that.'

'He'd only been married about two years, hadn't he?' he asked, in the tone used for steering sleepwalkers.

Maureen nodded. 'Yes. That's his first wife', she said, gesturing at Zena's photograph on the mantelpiece. 'She died of cancer.'

'And he married the present Mrs. Henham soon after, I believe?'

'About six months later. He had of course known her for longer than that', she added, in a tone which seemed to imply that it made all the difference between what was decent and what was tasteless.

'Was there much gossip at the time? About his remarriage, I mean?'

'Men like Mr. Henham are always a prey to gossip', she replied austerely.

Manton gravely pondered the ambiguity of this comment and then said:

'I suppose the present Mrs. Henham's divorce must have been going through about the same time as the first Mrs. Henham was dying.'

'That's what all the gossip was about.'

'Miss Fox, tell me something about his personal habits. For instance, was he tidy or untidy, punctual or unpunctual, even-tempered or the reverse?'

'He was an extremely orderly person. He always kept his briefs tidy and never mussed up all his papers the way most counsel do. He used to make the most wonderful notes of his cases and was a great one for keeping records. So much so, that he often used to dictate minutes of conversations to avoid any subsequent dispute about what had been said.'

'How very sensible, but it must have meant an awful lot of extra work for you.'

'Oh, I didn't have to transcribe all of them.' Then seeing the slightly puzzled expression on Manton's face, she said, 'He used this recording-machine and I only had to make a transcript if any query arose later.'

'I follow.' Manton studied the recording-machine for a while. It was a well-known make and he had used a similar type himself on many occasions. The dictation was recorded on a wafer-thin brown record. 'What did Mr. Henham do with the records which you weren't required to transcribe?' he suddenly asked and was quick to notice that the question caused Maureen to blush.

'I've no idea', she said, with ill-assumed nonchalance. 'I suppose he used to keep them somewhere or other.'

'But you don't know where?'

She shook her head and shrugged off the question. So Mr. Henham kept dictated records of his private views and thoughts, but Miss Fox didn't wish to discuss the subject. So be it, thought Manton. Aloud he said:

'Do you know whether Mr. Henham had any enemies?'

The sudden change of topic brought Maureen evident relief. 'I know that he and Mr. Justice Riley didn't get on too well', she replied. 'The judge is a nasty bit of goods. I reckon he's the enemy of a good many people.'

'Anyone else?'

'No.'

'What about his stepson?'

'Robin?' Her tone was derisory. 'He's just a silly jealous kid, who is full of talk. I suppose he's told you all

100

sorts of spiteful things about Mr. Henham.' Since this was said more as a statement of fact than as a question, Manton saw no need to correct the assumption.

'Finally, Miss Fox, I'd like to ask you about Mr. Henham's cough capsules. Did you ever buy them for him?'

'Often.'

'A recently bought tube was found in his pocket. Do you know where it came from?'

'I expect that was the one I took to him in court after the lunch adjournment. He sent a message asking me to get him some more.'

'And where did you buy them?'

'*I* didn't buy them. Robin, who brought me the message, also brought the capsules. He said he'd passed a chemist's and thought he'd save me the bother of getting them.' Her tone was scornful but suddenly her expression changed. 'Surely you don't think it was one of those which poisoned him?'

'Had it not struck you as a possibility?'

'Oh, how awful to think it might have been one of the capsules I emptied out for him.'

'*You* . . .'

'Yes, you see he'd hurt his hand and couldn't get the sealing tape round the cap off. He asked me to do it for him.'

'Did the capsules ever leave your possession between the time Robin King-Selman handed them to you and your giving them to Mr. Henham?'

Maureen shook her head. She seemed to be genuinely stunned by the possibility which had just been postulated.

'Do you remember – and this is most important – whether or not there were any capsules already on the desk when you brought him the fresh supply after lunch?'

'I'm almost sure there was one there – possibly two – no, one. Yes, I'm certain it was only one.'

Manton nodded his head thoughtfully. 'You're about to leave your job here, aren't you?'

'Mmm.'

'Of your own accord?'

'Mmm.'

'Does your departure have anything to do with Mr. Henham?'

The question was answered by Alfred Exley, who suddenly appeared in the doorway like the spirit of Aladdin's lamp. 'Hadn't you better tell the Superintendent that it was on Mr. Henham's instructions that you were given notice?'

Manton saw her eyes glint angrily and the muscles of her face harden and for one moment he thought she was going to hurl a handy inkpot at the clerk. Instead she suddenly crumpled up and dissolved into tears.

'Your problem, I'm afraid', he said heartlessly and made for the door.

As he walked across the hall, he heard Alfred Exley speaking in cold unsympathetic tones. 'You're just a lying little schemer, who'll come to a bad end.'

With a heavily preoccupied expression he walked up Middle Temple Lane. He'd learnt one interesting fact, anyway.

Robin King-Selman bounded up the final flight of stairs which led to his laboratory three at a time, his thick crêpe-soled shoes adding spring to his step. His stepfather's death only twenty-four hours before, although personally unmourned, had had a cathartic effect on him. In many ways, definable and indefinable, its suddenness had completely changed his world, so that even the staid Kensington street outside appeared subtly different and the tower on Campden Hill which quietly dominated the scene had become invested with a new significance.

The ultimate effect on Robin had been to make him fall back still further on to his own resources. Always a prey to intense introspection, any crisis in his life made him withdraw from his fellow-creatures as swiftly as the timidly questing head of a frightened tortoise.

On the top stair, he suddenly stopped. A shadow had fallen distinctly across the light which was reflected beneath the door. He felt his heart leap as he stood there listening and looking like an angular statue suddenly frozen in movement. He knew for certain that someone was in his laboratory; someone who had no right to be there. He had never been a young man who craved for excitement or who professed to yearn for opportunities of Bulldog Drummond stuff in the home. On the contrary, he cordially disliked all ideas of violence, even to the extent of once walking off the field during a game of mixed hockey and refusing further participation.

To his surprise, however, he suddenly found himself springing at the door and flinging it open with all the drama of poor but honest Jake showing his fallen daughter to the snow-drifts outside. He stood there off balance with the stiff appearance of a puppet, peering in but seeing no one. There was a movement and then from behind an ancient tallboy on which he kept a lot of his apparatus stepped Marcus King-Selman.

'Hello, Robin', he said in an odd tone of voice. 'I thought a hurricane must have hit the door. I never heard you come up the stairs.'

'What are you doing here?' Robin asked, looking as awkward as he sounded suspicious.

'As a matter of fact I was looking for you. I wanted to have a chat with you about what's happened.' For the first time in his life Marcus found himself being stared out of countenance by his son and felt distinctly ill at ease. The boy had a knack of looking at you with his

103

eyes very wide open which gave him a disconcertingly quizzical expression. 'Yes,' he faltered, 'how do you think your mother is bearing up?'

'She seems to be all right', Robin replied stolidly.

'You mustn't forget how much she relies on you at a time like this, Robin.'

'And you', Robin replied. His tone was sweet – too sweet – and studiously free of innuendo.

'Yes, of course, but there are reasons which make it difficult for me to help her as much as I would wish.' Up to this point the conversation had been conducted across the room but Marcus now came over to the door. 'You haven't forgotten all I said to you yesterday evening, have you? It's vitally important that you follow my instructions to the letter.' Though he spoke with heavy emphasis, Robin said nothing and Marcus would have given much at that moment to have enjoyed clairvoyant powers. 'Well, I must be on my way. Is your mother downstairs?'

'I expect so.'

'I'll look in anyway. See you again shortly.' And with that Marcus King-Selman disappeared from view down the stairs and Robin stepped thoughtfully into the laboratory and slowly closed the door behind him.

Helen Riley was alone in the house. It was Hislop's afternoon off and at lunch-time the judge had phoned to say that he would not be back for dinner till after eight o'clock. He had not given her any explanation and she had not asked for one, which was typical of the double-track state into which their marriage had developed.

Immediately after a frugal lunch, Helen had closeted herself in the kitchen and now moved about it humming softly to herself as she collected all the ingredients she required for cake-making. This was a favoured pastime when she was alone and one at which she excelled. She was equally proficient at sweet-making and before the war had usefully and substantially supplemented Gethin's allowance to her by selling her home-made chocolates to a small but exclusive shop, which used immediately to double the price and keep them for the real connoisseurs amongst its diet-resisting lady clients. On this particular afternoon she decided to make some meringues which happened to be one of her husband's more harmless passions.

While she worked with all the deft skill of an expert, her mind inevitably dwelt on Christopher's death. Though she had known him so long and flirted with him so recently, she could not but help feeling a sense of overwhelming relief at his removal. He had been very obstinate about the car accident and had seemed determined to involve her in a scandal whose proportions were likely to be as unpredictable as an atomic explosion, and as potentially disastrous. Obviously Gethin was quite right about his having blind spots.

She stopped humming and with great care added some essence to the creamy mixture. One drop too much and it'd be ruined: one too little and her husband would bitterly complain. As she started to stir again, her thoughts followed a new line and she resolved that as soon as she had finished, she would go and visit Celia. No sooner was this decided than her mind switched back to thoughts of Christopher. She accepted it as probable that the full shock of his death would hit her suddenly, but so far her sense of escape from imminent danger far outweighed any other emotion. She pondered the motives of self-preservation and reflected how they formed by far the most indestructible driving force in human relationships.

At last the meringues were in the oven where they

could be left gently baking till her return and she went up to her bedroom to get ready.

It was a lovely spring afternoon and she decided to walk to the Henhams' house, which was not more than half to three-quarters of a mile distant. Apart from a perilous crossing of Kensington High Street, her way lay along quiet roads whose houses showed few signs of life at that hour. From time to time the stale and unattractive odour of roast meat came floating up from a basement area, usually accompanied by the ominous sounds of china and cutlery jostling in a kitchen sink.

When Doris opened the drawing-room door and announced, 'Lady Riley to see you, mum', Celia was over at her writing-desk and found herself presented with the *fait accompli* of an unwanted visitor. This, however, was a deliberate tactic on Helen's part who had out-manœuvred Doris and gained the drawing-room without delay or obstruction.

The two women met in the middle of the room and pecked the air as their cheeks cruised past each other.

'My dear,' Helen began, 'I just had to come round and see you. Words are totally inadequate at a time like this but I do want you to know how much I'm with you in your crushing loss. It's one of the most appalling tragedies and that it should have happened to Christopher of all people.' The words were cloying, the sentiments conventional, and Celia listened with a sweetly sad expression and a completely detached mind. Helen went on, 'There must be something I can do for you, my dear. If not now, then later; and of course I speak for Gethin too.'

'It's very good of you to call, Helen. One's friends are a great source of comfort at such times as these. Do sit down and stay a little while.'

Helen had every intention of doing this and sat herself daintily on the sofa, smoothing her skirt as she did so. There was no doubt that she was, as always, superbly turned out for she had almost perfect taste in all things feminine. Celia, who had always recognized her inability to compete with her on matters of dress, found compensation in never missing an opportunity of stressing their difference in age, which was six years in her, Celia's, favour.

'Considering the ghastly shock it must have been to you, I think you've borne up wonderfully well', remarked Helen, with crackling brightness. 'But then you are a courageous woman. You must be to have been present there and seen Christopher collapse.'

'You speak as though I knew he was going to', Celia said sharply.

'Of course I don't mean that, my dear. But to have seen it all happen must have added to the shock.'

'It was a tremendous shock', agreed Celia, avoiding looking at Helen's trim figure on the sofa. 'And like such experiences, it's more unreal than real.'

'How lucky you've got Robin and – er – your previous husband to relieve you of all the administrative worries, wills and all the rest of it. Particularly as your . . . as Marcus looks such a very practical sort of man.' She gave Celia a little smile of sympathetic understanding and continued, 'It's akin to these fearful cases of negligence which one so often reads about these days.'

'What is?'

'Christopher's death', she replied, with a sad shake of her neat little head. 'I suppose some totally unqualified youth is responsible; left to concoct prescriptions without having the faintest idea what he's doing or of the lethal properties of the drugs he's mixing.'

'But you don't really think that Christopher died as a

107

result of someone's negligence?' Celia said, in a tone of genuine surprise.

'How else, my dear?'

'By someone deliberately poisoning him.'

'You can't mean that, Celia. It's just too fantastic. Who would do such a thing?'

'That's for the police to find out, if they can. I'm quite certain *they* have no illusions about it. *They* know that Christopher was murdered.'

'How ghastly.' Helen's voice was only a whisper and she grimaced as if she'd just bitten into a lemon. 'Of course that explains . . .' The sentence trailed away unfinished and she looked up at Celia to find her watching her closely. 'My dear, I hardly know what to say . . . have *you* any idea who might have done such a wicked thing?'

Celia paused before shaking her head and saying, 'It must have been someone who knew about his habit of taking things for his throat.'

'But that narrows it down to his friends – and family.'

'Precisely. I imagine we're all under suspicion, though some no doubt to a greater degree than others.'

'My dear, not only to have lost your husband but to be suspected of having murdered him; it's too awful. I don't know why you're not demented by it all.'

'But I didn't say that *I* was suspected.'

'No, of course they can't suspect you', replied Helen, without any attempt at conviction.

'Tell me this, Helen', Celia said, speaking slowly and deliberately. 'Were you in the car with Christopher that evening when he had the accident?'

The colour drained from Helen's face and she gripped the arm of the sofa. For Celia, her question had already been answered. 'I thought you were. You'll be able to come and give evidence for me at the Old Bailey in a fortnight's time.'

Helen managed to regain control of her floundering emotions and thoughts.

'The strain has been too much for you, my dear', she said. 'It's quite unthinkable that they'll still go on with your case. It would be refined cruelty to do so.' She paused. 'Now that is something I probably can do for you. I'll get Gethin to have a word with someone about it – the Lord Chief Justice or the Attorney-General.' She got up and pulled on her gloves. 'I must be going, my dear. Why don't you go and lie down? You must be desperately tired.' She started to walk to the door and suddenly turned back. With her head cocked slightly on one side and an oddly disconcerting expression about her mouth and eyes, she surveyed Celia and seemed to be about to say something, something which wouldn't trip as easily from her tongue as her earlier conversation. Celia found herself waiting in taut expectation and then suddenly the moment had passed and she afterwards wondered if she hadn't imagined it. Helen gave her a quick smile, and a further conventional word of leave-taking and departed.

Manton sat back comfortably in the judge's seat in Divorce Court No. 5A. Sergeant Talper was prowling about in the rows reserved for counsel, but otherwise the court was empty. It was shortly after five o'clock and the cataracts of forensic oratory which gush through the Royal Courts of Justice for approximately four and a half to five hours each day (Saturdays and Sundays excepted) had been stemmed till half-past ten the following morning. The judges had gone off to their clubs for a cup of tea and the rest of the courts' working population to their lawful though less innocent pursuits.

'I reckon', said Manton, gazing about him like a sightseer, 'that the chap who designed this court must have journeyed with Orpheus in the underworld.'

'Like all our courts', said Talper vigorously. 'They're either historic and uncomfortable or modern and soft to the seat.'

'That may apply to most of the Assize Courts, but there's precious little historic about this one despite its discomfort. Hello, what's this?' he added, leaning forward and picking up a small tin from the judge's desk. 'Umujubes, eh?' He opened it and grunted.

'What's in it, sir?'

'Paper clips and a razor blade.' He got up and joined Talper at the solicitors' table in the well of the court. Sitting down on it, he rested his feet on the hard narrow bench where solicitors were wont to squirm in silent discomfort, which was either aggravated or mitigated by the performance of the counsel whom they were instructing. After a thoughtful pause, he said, 'Correct me if I go wrong, Andy, but isn't this the story.

'During the lunch adjournment Mr. Justice Riley presses some Umujubes on to Mr. Henham and tells him to take them instead of his own capsules. In the course of the afternoon, Henham gets one of his coughing fits and the judge urges him to take a Umujube. He does so – or rather, he appears to do so – and soon after drops dead. Correct so far?'

Sergeant Talper nodded. 'There is one point, sir. You remember yesterday evening when we were discussing the case you mentioned the possibility of the judge having been an innocent agent. Well, Mr. Quirkly, the counsel who accompanied Mr. Henham to the judge's room, has stated that he quite clearly recalls that it was Lady Riley who suggested that Mr. Henham should try her husband's lozenges.'

'That's significant.'

'Except, how, if it was she who planted the poisoned Umujube on her husband, was she to know that he would pass that particular one to the deceased?'

'Perhaps', Manton said thoughtfully, 'she meant to poison her husband and not Henham.'

'In that event why urge him to dish out Umujubes amongst which, for all she knew, might be the carefully poisoned one?'

Manton smiled. 'I don't think I can find you an answer to that question – at any rate not for the moment. Now let us go a stage further. If it was a poisoned Umujube, then at least two people had opportunity to fix it. The judge *and* his wife. I think we can almost certainly include her. Agreed? Good. On the other hand if it was a poisoned capsule, it must have come from one of two different sources. Either from the tube bought during the lunch adjournment by Robin King-Selman, who be it noted was never asked to make the purchase but did so gratuitously, and handed it to Maureen Fox who in turn gave it to the deceased, opening it, as she says, in his presence. Or it was the lonely one left over from the morning's supply about which at the moment we know nothing. However, provided we ask the right person or persons, we should be able to find out quite easily where and when that lot was bought.'

'How do you mean, sir, right person?'

'This shows all the signs of being a family affair. If we ask the wrong member of the family, i.e. the murderer, we shan't get the truth.'

'But family rules out the judge.'

'Oh, no. I count him and his wife. After all they've all known each other for years and got neighbouring cottages in the country.' He thoughtfully tapped his teeth with the nail of his left index finger. 'So I

111

don't think that we'll ask Mrs. Henham about it', he added.

'What about motive?' Talper asked.

'Yes, indeed. Who had a motive? There we're on far less certain ground. Wives often do have motives (very good ones, too) for murdering their husbands, but we don't know of any particular one that Mrs. Henham had. They'd only been married two years and from all accounts she'd gone to a fair degree of trouble to net her man. We shall have to dig deep, Andy. Her ex-husband provides more promising material as a motive breeding-ground. After all, Mrs. Henham made him give her a divorce which, with true cricketing spirit, he did. But he doesn't appear to bear her any ill-will and one can properly infer that he's still in love with her; with converse feelings toward the man who stole her from him. As for Master Robin, I gather from Maureen Fox that he didn't get on very well with his stepfather but that's hardly in itself sufficient reason to kill him. Then we come to the judge, who seems to have a cordial dislike of all his fellow-creatures, the sentiment being fully reciprocated. He'd known the deceased for over a quarter of a century and Mrs. Henham is quite certain that it was he who murdered her husband from some deep mystery motive of the past. And the judge's wife? We must find out some more about her.

'Well, there are our suspects and their motives. You can take your pick.'

The swing doors of the court opened at that moment and a young plain-clothes detective officer came in. He had been waiting in the police car in the quadrangle below.

'A message has just come over the blower, sir. It's from the lab. Definite traces of Umujube have been found in the deceased's stomach contents.'

'That's a positive step in a certain direction', said Manton. Sergeant Talper gave a low whistle.

'You here again?' said the plump Doris, on opening the door and seeing Manton. She then noticed Talper. 'Brought a boy-friend with you this time, I see. I'm afraid the missus is out. Mr. King-Selman came for her about twenty minutes ago.'

'I really wanted to see Mr. Robin', Manton said agreeably, correctly assuming that Doris's reference to Mr. King-Selman had been to Marcus.

'Oh, he's upstairs in his laboratory. You can find your own way up, can't you? Them stairs gives me such puffs and jelly knees. Besides, I'd like to get back to my comp.'

'Yes, we can manage all right. How are you getting on with Marilyn Monroe's undies?'

'Oh, I've finished that one. This next one's real good though. You has to pick the best table decorations for a banquet at Buckingham Palace and the first prize is to appear on T.V. with Lady Something or other *and* get a pressure cooker.'

'You'll have to find a husband to go with all these pressure cookers, you know', Manton said with a smile. He moved toward the staircase. 'Don't bother about us, we'll find our way out again.'

'Okey dokey', said Doris, and ambled away toward the kitchen and her comp.

'And I suppose that lump costs them about three quid a week', Sergeant Talper said scornfully as they mounted the stairs. 'And just so that they can boast of a resident staff.'

'Listen to Comrade Talper. Down with privilege and the capitalist classes. For all information apply to Room 4824, New Scotland Yard. Subversive activities on easy terms.'

113

'Well,' said Talper with stolid good humour, 'I don't feel Eva and I are missing much by not having one of the likes of dainty Doris about our house. But I suppose it's all a matter of taste.'

They arrived at the laboratory door. Manton knocked and entered without waiting for a reply. Robin was sitting at a table by the window poring over a book. It was evident that he hadn't heard them come in and Manton noisily cleared his throat. He immediately looked up and started from his chair in surprise and confusion, hastily closing the book behind him with a clumsy gesture.

'Good evening, Mr. King-Selman', said Manton pleasantly. 'I'm Detective-Superintendent Manton of Scotland Yard and this is Detective-Sergeant Talper.' Robin jerked his head in acknowledgement of the introduction and Manton continued, 'This is a nice laboratory you've got fitted out up here.' He walked round the room, casting a quick appraising glance at the various bottles and jars on the shelves.

He turned to face Robin and said,' There's one particular thing I want to ask you about, Mr. King-Selman. I believe that yesterday you bought your stepfather a tube of Capstick's Cough Capsules. That is right, isn't it?'

'Yes, why not?' Robin answered nervously.

'Did he ask you to get them for him?'

'Well, yes and no. Actually he asked me to tell Miss Fox to buy them, but as I happened to pass a chemist's, I thought I'd save her the trouble.'

'In that event, why didn't you hand them to your stepfather yourself?'

'I don't understand . . .'

'Why give them to a third person to give him when you were going to see him yourself anyway?'

114

'Because . . . well . . . because he hadn't asked me to get them and was expecting Miss Fox to bring them to him in court after lunch.'

Manton felt that his question was not receiving a very satisfactory answer.

'And you bought the capsules at the chemist's opposite the Law Courts?' he asked.

'Yes, but how do you know?' Robin's voice had a note of alarm.

'It's my job to know these things. Is there any chance that the tube you bought got swapped with another?'

'What other?'

Manton sighed. 'Are you quite sure that the tube of capsules which you handed to Miss Fox was the same one which you bought at the chemist's?'

Robin gulped. 'Of course I'm sure', he said with a trace of defiance in his tone.

'And you never opened it while it was in your possession?'

'No, why should I have?'

'I only asked you and you tell me, no. So be it. Now tell me this. Do you keep any potassium cyanide up here?'

Robin's face went a waxy white and for one moment he looked as though he might be going to pitch face forwards on to the floor.

'Yes, I have a very little', he said in a barely audible whisper.

'May I see it please?'

Robin went to one of the shelves and started to peer earnestly along it. Then putting up a hand he picked up a number of the receptacles, only to replace them again. He was clearly becoming increasingly agitated and when he eventually turned and faced the two officers, his expression was that of a thoroughly scared young man.

'It's gone', he said hoarsely.

'Are you certain?' Manton asked sharply.

'Yes. It was here on this shelf. Oh, my God, this is awful', he moaned, and slumped heavily into a chair.

CHAPTER TWELVE

STILL in a daze, Robin found himself being driven with skill and speed toward Scotland Yard. He had been in no condition to object when Manton suggested with some firmness that the interview should be continued under that roof, and now as he sat in the car gazing distractedly at the back of Sergeant Talper's head, he gave the complete appearance of one being rushed to the Lubianka prison for a final bout of pre-confession persuasion.

Not even the driver's scrupulous regard for old ladies on pedestrian crossings and his friendly wink at a pretty bus conductress could mitigate his sensation of nightmarish doom.

As the car turned off Whitehall and came to a halt in the courtyard, Manton got out.

'This way, Mr. King-Selman', he said holding the door open for Robin. As they entered the building, Sergeant Talper fell in at the rear, and any ideas that Robin might have had of sudden wild flight were stifled. 'Do sit down and make yourself as comfortable as you can, Mr. King-Selman', Manton said when they finally reached his office. 'Now to continue. When did you last see the potassium cyanide in your laboratory?'

Robin meanwhile had decided to try and please his captors in the faint hope that they would let him go in a reasonable state of repair and not hold him *incomunicado* in their dungeons for an indefinite period. His hazy knowledge of the law of habeas corpus and of police procedure was an indifferently distilled blend of the *News of the World*, a book he had recently read on Nazi oppression and the works of a well-known crime writer whose fictional Yard officers enjoyed extravagant powers over their hapless victims which always led to dramatic solutions and orgies of strictly poetic justice.

'When I brought it back from the cottage last Sunday', he replied.

'There's some down there?'

'It's in the garden shed. We got it last year to deal with wasps' nests and there was quite a lot left over.'

'And there's still some there?'

'Oh, yes, I only took a very little.'

'What did you want it for?'

'Because . . . well, simply because I hadn't got any in my laboratory.'

'Did you have any particular use for it in mind?'

'No, definitely not.'

'And yet you took the trouble to bring it back?'

'Yes. You see . . . you must see that as a chemistry student, I like to have as many different things as possible in my laboratory.'

'Did anyone know that you had brought it back?'

'Er – no . . . at least, yes. Sir Gethin Riley was in the garden shed when I took it.'

'I see. Who goes into your laboratory apart from yourself?'

'No one, really.'

'But I presume that anyone can?'

'Oh, yes, I don't keep the door locked or anything like that.'

'And this potassium cyanide has disappeared sometime between last Sunday and now?'

'It must have.'

'You know, of course, that your stepfather died as a result of potassium cyanide poisoning?'

'No, no, I didn't know. I swear I didn't', Robin replied, bobbing with agitation.

'Didn't you? At any rate, you now realize what a very serious matter the disappearance of this poison is?'

Robin nodded his head energetically.

'Do you know where your stepfather used to buy his cough capsules?' Manton asked abruptly.

'I don't think he got them at any one particular shop.'

'Do you happen to know where he bought those he was swallowing on the morning of the trial – that is, the last lot he had before you bought him a final tube at lunch that day?'

'I believe he got them on his way home the previous evening.'

'You believe?'

'That's what my mother told me later.'

Manton and Talper exchanged a quick glance.

'How did she know?'

'Apparently he couldn't unscrew the top – you see he'd hurt his hand – and he asked my mother to do so.'

'And she did?'

'Actually, no. She couldn't either and it was my father who finally unscrewed it.'

'You weren't present when this happened?'

'No.'

'But you were told all about it afterwards?'

'Yes', Robin said uncomfortably.

'Did your mother ever refer in your presence to her motor accident?' Manton asked, once more switching the subject without warning.

'Well – er – well yes, in a way I suppose she did.'

'Did she ever suggest that in fact it wasn't she who was driving at the time?'

119

Robin suddenly went very white and his mouth opened like a fish taking in air.

'Well, did she?' pressed Manton.

'Yes.'

'When?'

'The same day that the summons was served on her.'

'Do you know whether she told anyone else?'

'My father knew. He was there at the time.' Robin now looked bitterly ill at ease.

'In the car?' asked Manton sharply.

'No, at the cottage when my mother told us about it.'

'Do you know who *was* driving at the time?'

'My stepfather.'

'That's what your mother told you?'

'Yes.'

'Was your mother very upset by the manslaughter proceedings against her?'

'Yes.'

'And doubtless felt that your stepfather had badly let her down?'

'Yes, I suppose so.' Robin's replies were coming automatically, almost as if he were acting under an hypnotic drug.

'And I suppose you and Mr. Marcus King-Selman took the same view?'

'Yes, my father was furious and . . .' Robin's Adam's apple gobbled wildly and he abruptly left the sentence unfinished.

'. . . And . . . was generally very ill-disposed toward your stepfather about it, I dare say', said Manton quickly. There was no reply and he continued, 'Well, I think we'll get all this down in statement form. Sergeant Talper, would you take Mr. King-Selman along to your room and take a written statement from him.' He opened the door and ushered Robin out into the corridor. As Talper followed him, Manton put out a detaining hand and whispered, 'We're progressing on motives anyway.'

Hardly had he closed the door and sat down again at his desk, when Talper came back in.

'I thought I'd just mention, sir, that that book our young friend shut so smartly when we surprised him in his lab. was Glaister's *Medical Jurisprudence and Toxicology.*'

'I suppose there's nothing very significant in a chemistry student reading that', Manton replied.

'When he shut the book in that hurry, the page he'd been reading got bent back', continued Talper in his maddeningly stolid way.

'I see. Well?'

'It was the page dealing with symptoms of poisoning by potassium cyanide.'

Celia and Marcus had returned home and Celia's first act was to light a cigarette, then remove her hat and throw it into the corner of the sofa, where it lay looking like a mangled bird.

'Aren't you smoking rather too much?' asked Marcus.

'Probably, but that's my look-out.'

'Please don't talk like that, dear. You know how much I —'

'Yes, Marcus,' Celia broke in, 'I know how much you say you love me.'

'That's a beastly spiteful thing to say.'

'Well, I'm sorry, but I do sometimes doubt whether you love me as much as you pretend. After all, you surrendered me to Christopher without putting up very much of a fight. In fact I don't remember your fighting at all.'

Marcus assumed the expression of a sorely tried saint having to cope with a fractious sinner at the end of a particularly tiring day. 'I'm not going to let you provoke me,' he said, 'because I know you don't mean what you're saying. But I must urge you not to let yourself go to pieces at this critical juncture in our affairs. The situation is far too tricky and dangerous.'

Celia got up and paced restlessly across to the window.

'Oh, I can't bear it, here are the police again', she suddenly cried out. 'How I hate the sight of their sleek, black cars.' A further startled exclamation brought Marcus to her side. 'My God, it's Robin.' Marcus was in time to see their son shoot out of the car as though propelled by unseen hands. But almost before they had fully taken in the scene, the front door slammed and there were racing footsteps up the stairs. The car, in considerably less haste, pulled silently away from the kerb and disappeared down the street.

Celia at once dashed out of the room after her son. Marcus was about to follow but had second thoughts and instead went across to the cocktail cabinet and poured himself out a drink.

'Well?' he asked when Celia returned to the drawing-room two minutes later.

'He's locked himself in his bedroom and refuses to open the door.'

'Did he speak to you?'

'Only to say he'd come down soon.' She turned to her ex-husband appealingly. 'Oh, Marcus, I'm worried about him.'

'So am I', he replied in a cheerless tone. As he spoke, he started to pace the room and Celia could see that his mind was on other things. His brow was furrowed and he flicked his fingers noisily so that she felt like screaming at him to stop. She was also getting tired of finding herself in the midst of conspiratorial silences. First it was with Helen, now with Marcus.

'Do stop wearing a trail in the carpet,' she said at last, adding, 'and flicking your fingers in that childish way.'

He came over to where she was sitting. 'I'm worried about you, Celia', he said solemnly.

'Oh?' She couldn't be bothered to sound interested.

He ignored the discouraging note in her voice and went on, 'I think you may be in danger; that there might be an attempt on your life.'

'What? Someone try and murder me?' she asked, as though struck by the novelty of the idea.

He nodded and she turned away with a gesture of exasperation.

'Don't forget that someone deliberately poisoned your husband', he persisted, watching her closely.

'Do you want me to employ a food taster then? Do you imagine we're back with the Borgias?'

'This is no time for sarcasm.'

'Nor for idiotic suggestions.'

His cheeks flamed as he suddenly turned on his heel and strode out of the room, leaving Celia to stare angrily after him.

The muted chimes of the hall clock were sounding half past eight as Mr. Justice Riley turned his key in the latch and stepped across the threshold of his home. Helen, who was *en route* from kitchen to dining-room, paused as she heard the door open.

'Hello, Gethin, you're back.'

Superfluous observations of this sort always irritated the judge and it was with asperity that he replied.

'It's half past eight and you may recall that I said I'd be back at that hour.'

'Yes, and dinner is ready. It's a cold collation as Hislop is out.'

'So I presumed. She always is on Wednesday evenings.'

'Well, hurry up and have a wash. I've got something to discuss with you.'

He eyed his wife impassively as he gently sucked an Umujube and then slowly stumped up the stairs.

As soon as they were seated at table, Helen said, 'I went to see Celia Henham this afternoon.'

'One moment', replied the judge, getting up. 'You don't seem to have laid the sugar and tomato soup always requires it.' With maddening deliberation he walked across to the sideboard, fetched the sugar and returned to his seat. 'Yes, you were saying you paid a call on Celia Henham this afternoon. How is she reacting to her husband's death?'

'On the whole she seemed to be remarkably composed. But the point is this, she knows I was out with Christopher on the evening of the accident.'

'Did Christopher tell her?'

'I don't know. She didn't say. I suppose he must have done, though I'm surprised.'

'And what use is she going to make of the information?'

'She merely said I'd be able to give evidence for her at the Old Bailey.'

'And what did you say to that?' asked the judge, fiercely crumbling a piece of bread on his side plate.

'I didn't. I changed the subject. I never admitted I was in the car.'

'Other than by your conduct, you mean.'

'I don't think my conduct imported guilt.'

'Be that as it may, the fact remains that there is still someone alive who knows the truth', he said thoughtfully. Helen glanced at him sharply.

'Surely they won't still try her for manslaughter? Not after all this?' she said.

'What has a piece of disgraceful driving in Gloucester Road got to do with the poisoning of a divorce counsel in court? Of course her trial will go on.'

'Couldn't you speak to someone about it? The Attor-

124

ney-General or the Director of Public Prosecutions or whoever it is can quash proceedings?'

Mr. Justice Riley pursed his lips and pushed his soup plate away from him. 'It certainly seems that something will have to be done', he said, and immediately became submerged in deep thought. As Helen placed a plate of cold ham and tongue before him, he added, 'Christopher may be dead but his voice almost certainly is not.'

'What on earth do you mean?'

Eyeing the ham with apparent disfavour, he replied, 'I refer to his habit of making recorded notes of such incidents as this motoring affair. The odds are that somewhere in Chambers a record exists. Mmmm – pass me the salad dressing, would you please?' Helen watched him plaster his food with the prodigality of a slapstick team engaged in an act with buckets of whitewash. 'In the circumstances, Christopher's death appears to have left us as vulnerable as we were before it.' After a further pause, he went on, 'I know, my dear, that you are fonder of your position than you are of your husband, but at the moment it so happens that we share a common interest – the interest of self-preservation. Any breath of scandal will not only be extremely damaging to my career as a judge but it will utterly ruin yours as a judge's wife. Do I make myself clear?'

Helen met his eyes without a quaver and, apart from heightened colour about her cheek-bones, she gave no indication of having heard anything remotely untoward.

'Yes, Gethin, you make things very clear', she said at last. 'But as you say, this is a time for solidarity, so shall we now discuss practical steps and try and reach a decision on our next move?'

'Yes', replied the judge, buttering a baked potato with obvious relish. 'We will do that now, for time is not on our side.'

CHAPTER THIRTEEN

M ANTON had hardly stepped into his office the following
morning when he received a summons to the Commissioner's room.

'Well?' said the great man, as Manton closed the door
behind him. 'It's over thirty-six hours since I gave you
your dangerous assignment, what have you to report?
I may add that I didn't bother you yesterday, though I
had the Attorney-General, the Home Office and the Lord
Chancellor's Department all dancing on the line like a lot
of agitated hens.' He chuckled. 'I managed to fob them
off for the time being but I must have something to tell
them to-day.'

For the next twenty minutes Manton related the course
of his inquiry to date. He omitted nothing and made his
account factual with the minimum intrusion of personal
comment. When he had finished, the Commissioner sat
back in his chair, took off his spectacles and polished them
carefully with a grubby piece of blotting-paper.

'I take it that you're not yet in any position to put your
suspects in a particular order?' he said at last.

'No, I suppose not, sir', Manton replied cautiously.

'Though there's much to point to the judge as number
one.'

'But no motive, sir.'

'But no motive', echoed the Commissioner sadly.
Then after a pause he continued, 'I'm impressed by the
possibility that the judge might have been an innocent

agent in palming off the poisoned Umujube – perhaps it's just that I'm too conservative to be able to envisage an English High Court judge committing murder in his own court. But if he was an innocent agent, the chances are that it was his wife who so used him; though, once again, you've not uncovered any motive against her either.'

'That's so, sir.'

'Supposing she did have a motive and did murder Christopher Henham by getting her husband to give him a jujube which she had previously loaded with potassium cyanide, he would only glean the truth after the event. Correct?'

'Yes, sir.'

'And he might then well react as he has done. Not an easy position for any husband to be in, let alone one who is a High Court judge to boot.'

Manton sat quietly, not knowing whether the Commissioner's theorizing was at an end or merely being re-stoked. It was the latter.

'But we mustn't forget that you've found a strong motive against Mrs. Henham and one which also fits the son and ex - husband; menfolk - rallying - to - the - memsahib - in - trouble stuff. What I don't follow is this. Here was this fellow, Henham, sending for you last week and telling you that the manslaughter charge against his wife was false and that he's the guilty party – and making it all sound most improbable – when the whole problem could have been much more easily resolved with his wife's support.'

'I don't think, sir, I should have been any more impressed by the story, even if Mrs. Henham had been present to back it up. It would have needed more than their two words to convince me.'

'Maybe, but you'd better go through that manslaughter file with a fine tooth comb to see if you can't find some vital clue hidden away there.'

127

'I will, sir. I agree that the whole episode is pitted with unrealities . . . I mean, why didn't Mrs. Henham mention it when I saw her the evening before last? In the whole of our interview there wasn't one breath of a suggestion that the manslaughter case against her was unfounded; not one shadow of a word to that effect.'

'Yes, it's all extremely odd', said the Commissioner, with a heavy sigh. 'But I don't doubt that you will get sense out of it in the end.'

'If I don't, sir, it won't be for want of trying.'

'What about this girl in Chambers, do you really regard her as a suspect?'

'I do until I can exclude her, sir.' Then after a thoughtful pause Manton added emphatically, 'Yes, I most definitely regard her as a suspect.'

Celia closed her bedroom door softly and tiptoed across the room to the small bedside table which separated the two single beds. Sitting on the edge of her own bed, she gently lifted the telephone receiver and listened for a brief moment before dialling a number.

'Hello, is that Chambers? This is Mrs. Henham speaking.' She kept her voice low as though afraid of being overheard and went on, 'Is Mr. Exley there? . . . Oh . . . Is that Miss Fox? . . . I was ringing up, Miss Fox, because I wanted to come along to Chambers some time and go through my husband's things.'

At the other end of the line Maureen Fox caught her breath and said with a rush, 'I've got something awfully important *I*'d like to talk to *you* about, Mrs. Henham. It really is very important indeed', she repeated with increased emphasis. 'I was wondering if we could meet soon. Couldn't you come to Chambers this evening: after everyone has gone, I mean? Then I could help you with Mr. Henham's things and we could talk at the same time.' She finished breathlessly and for a space there was silence as Celia pondered the suggestion.

'Well, I suppose that would be all right', she said doubtfully, at last. 'Will you tell Mr. Exley?'

'Oh, no, Mrs. Henham, I can't possibly do that. He'd want to know everything.'

'All right, Miss Fox, I'll come along around half past eight this evening.'

'Thank you so much, Mrs. Henham. I'm sorry to sound so mysterious but I'd sooner not say any more on the phone.'

'All right. Good-bye.'

'Good-bye, Mrs. Henham. Thank you again for saying you'll come.'

As Maureen rang off, Celia heard a tell-tale little click. So someone had started listening in to her telephone calls now, had they, she mused as she replaced the receiver. It could only be Marcus or Robin.

When Maureen got back to Chambers after lunch, she found to her surprise a message asking her to ring Mr. Marcus King-Selman at his hotel. She observed that it was in the Strand less than ten minutes' walk away. After considerable contemplation she shrugged her shoulders and decided that she would let him phone again. He never did.

Instead at half past three Robin telephoned to suggest that he should take her out that evening. She told him curtly that he couldn't and rang off while he was still urging her to change her mind.

Marcus King-Selman had dined early and was pacing restlessly up and down his hotel bedroom like an expectant father. When the bedside telephone rang, he positively leapt toward it, as if fully expecting it to take to flight and elude his grasp.

'Is that Mr. King-Selman?'

'Yes, yes.'

'This is Miss Fox. Can you come to Chambers in about half an hour's time, Mr. King-Selman? It's something to do with Mr. Henham's death. It's . . .'

'Don't say any more now', he said and, slamming down the receiver with one hand, seized his raincoat with the other. The next moment, however, he quickly steadied himself and it was with a thoughtful expression that he watched himself in the wardrobe mirror doing up the buttons.

Just before eight o'clock Robin also answered the telephone and felt his heart leap as he recognized Maureen's voice and further leap as he detected a new and unusual note of vibrant excitement in her tone.

'Robin, you must come to Chambers immediately. Something terribly important in connection with your stepfather's death has just come to light and there's not a moment to be lost. You understand? Come now, straight away.'

'But what . . .'

'Don't start asking questions, Robin', she cut in tersely. 'But you must come.'

'Yes, all right.' With brain racing and heart pounding, he dropped the telephone receiver and dashed for the door.

Mr. Justice Riley sat in a deep arm-chair in his study moodily surveying the opposite wall. His expression was that of a Wagnerian neo-God brooding over an unreal calm before the final cataclysmic storm. He had just dined alone as Helen had pleaded a severe headache on his return home at six and had immediately retired to her room, leaving him to his own devices and a tray of cold supper. He didn't like dining early and intended protesting to her about it at a later date. Eight o'clock to eight-thirty was the only civilized hour at which to sit down to one's dinner and to have it at seven-twenty-five, as he had this evening, was repellently bourgeois and quite unendurable. Hislop had been off duty the previous evening and he could see no reason why she should be allowed out again tonight. Even if Helen didn't want any food, that was no reason why he should be rushed through his meal merely in order to allow their hired servant to go out and enjoy herself.

Thus he fumed, so that when the telephone rang it was some moments before he slowly put out a hand to answer it.

'Sir Gethin Riley speaking', he announced coldly.

'This is Miss Fox of Chambers, Sir Gethin. Something terribly important concerning Mr. Henham's death has just come to light. Could you come along at once, please?'

'Where are you speaking from?'

'From Chambers. You can tell how urgent it is, since I would never otherwise have dreamt of calling you. Please come at once.' The voice sounded oddly emotional and continued, 'Hello, are you still there?'

'Of course I'm still here. Now look here, young lady . . .'

'Oh, please don't start making difficulties.' Then, very slowly, she said, 'It's something which affects you most vitally.'

There was silence as the judge gave the matter cool but rapid thought and then suddenly down the line came a piercing cry of 'Help . . . Oh, what are you doing?' This was swiftly followed by a number of muffled thuds and bumps and in their midst Helen's voice suddenly cut in. She was not, it seemed, despite her indisposition, too incurious to listen in on her bedroom extension, reflected her husband acidly.

131

'For heaven's sake what's happening, Gethin? ... Miss Fox! Miss Fox!' There was no reply and Helen hurried on, 'It almost sounded as though she was being attacked. I'm sure something awful must have happened.'

'She's probably only fainted', he said.

'But I'm certain somebody else was there', said Helen in agitated tones. 'You must go round and see, Gethin.' He started to protest, though without conviction, and she impatiently brushed his words aside. 'Oh, do hurry.'

He sat motionless for a moment, his knuckles glistening as he gripped the receiver. 'Hello, hello', he repeated softly in urgent tones. 'Hello, is anyone there?' But now all was silent from the other end save for an indeterminate sound which might have been telephone atmospherics or something more human. With sudden decision he got up and left the room. In the hall he put on his hat and coat.

'I'm going now', he called out testily up the stairs and emerged from the house just in time to hail a passing taxi. Probably the silly girl had only had a fainting attack and yet he couldn't forget the shrill terror in that cry '. . . what are you doing?'

It was five and twenty minutes past eight as Helen hurried through the maze of passages which are the life veins of the Temple. She arrived at Christopher's block and ran up the stairs to his Chambers on the first floor. The front door was ajar and without knocking she entered. A light shone through the open door of Christopher's room and she half-ran across the hallway to it. On the floor by the desk lay Maureen Fox, her battered head in a pool of thick, congealing blood. Standing over her with a dazed expression on his face was Robin. In his hand was a heavily blood-stained poker.

CHAPTER FOURTEEN

'SHE's dead', said Robin, flatly. Although he had given no previous indication of being aware of Helen's presence, he now turned and looked in her direction. Her attention, however, still seemed to be riveted on the gruesome tableau and she didn't appear to hear him speak. It was the sound of footsteps coming up the stairs that finally brought them both back to reality; but before they had time to do anything, Celia appeared in the doorway.

She looked first at Maureen's crumpled body with wide unbelieving eyes and then at Robin, who was still holding the poker loosely at his side.

'Robin', she cried in a strangulated tone, 'Robin, my darling, for God's sake tell me what's happened? And Helen, what are you doing here?'

'Don't you think I'd better ring for the police, Celia?' Helen said. She looked at the telephone on Christopher's desk and continued, 'I'll go and do it from the main switchboard in the clerks' office.' She was about to leave the room when she turned back and added, 'We oughtn't to touch anything in here.' She spoke with the quiet authority which at any other time Celia would have found riling. As it was, she scarcely noticed the tone and barely comprehended the admonition.

As Helen was making her telephone call to Scotland Yard, she heard a man's voice in the hallway and peered round the door to see that Marcus had arrived. She

133

frowned but at that moment was connected with Manton.

'This is Lady Riley speaking, Superintendent. A terrible thing has happened. We've just arrived at Chambers to discover Miss Fox dead. She's been murdered. . . . You'll come at once? . . . Yes, I'll keep them all here till you arrive.'

She rejoined the others in Christopher's room. She noticed that the poker now lay on the floor beside Maureen and that Robin was sitting on an upright chair with his head supported by his hands and his eyes gazing unseeingly at Maureen's body. Celia was beside him trying to coax his attention and Marcus stood with his hand lightly resting on her shoulder in a statuesque pose. But Celia seemed to be totally unaware of her ex-husband's presence as she concentrated everything on making contact with her son, who more than ever resembled someone fallen into a mystic trance.

'I wonder where my husband has got to', Helen said in a puzzled tone. 'He left the house before I did.' Though the remark was addressed to no one in particular, both Marcus and Celia turned sharply and looked at her in silent astonishment.

The car bearing Manton and Talper to the scene of the crime turned off the Embankment and scraped through the narrow entrance of Middle Temple Lane. A few moments later it halted outside Christopher's Chambers with that sudden pneumatic lurch which is peculiar to police cars (real and fictional) drawing up outside the scenes of crimes. Instead, however, of flinging themselves out on to the pavement before the car came to a stop (as per fiction), Manton and Talper emerged with safety and decorum. A moment later they were in Christopher's room and the eyes of the four living occupants were turned upon them. Manton immediately went over to Maureen and knelt beside her, taking care to avoid the pool of blood which surrounded her head. After a brief scrutiny, he got up again.

'Get the photographic and fingerprint people along, Sergeant Talper.' Then he turned to face his avidly-watching audience. 'Has anyone touched anything?' he asked. No one answered, but Helen looked meaningly in Robin's direction. Manton noticed her expression. 'Yes, Lady Riley, I gather you have something you want to say.'

'Well, not me really', Helen said with hesitation. 'The point is I think Robin King-Selman er . . . moved something. Didn't you, Robin?' she added coaxingly.

'What?' he asked dully.

'Have you touched anything in this room?' asked Manton severely.

He shook his head.

'The poker', prompted Helen in an explosive hiss. At this, Celia gave her a look of cold loathing, which caused her to add, 'It's no good, my dear. It's bound to come out and it's much best that it should do so now – from Robin himself.'

'When I got here, I found Maureen dead and I picked up the poker', said Robin, finally coming in on his cue.

'That's right,' Helen said encouragingly, 'and I must have arrived soon after because I found you standing over her still holding it.'

'I see', said Manton, scribbling rapidly in a small note-book.

'The photograph and fingerprint people are on their way, sir', said Sergeant Talper, suddenly reappearing.

'Good.' Then addressing them all, Manton continued, 'I want you to come into one of the other rooms, and we'll continue this inquiry. Sergeant, will you please ring up the clerk to the Chambers and tell him what's hap-

pened. You'd also better get through to the head of
Chambers and tell him. Incidentally who is it now that
Mr. Henham is dead?' There was no reply and he concluded, 'Anyway it'll be the next name down of those
painted on the wall outside.'

'Very good, sir', replied Talper, and departed once
more.

'Right, we'll now go into the other room. Will you
lead on, Lady Riley?'

Helen got up from her chair and was about to move
across to the door when she suddenly stopped dead.
Manton followed the line of her gaze and saw, standing
in the doorway looking as if he'd materialized from a
trap-door in the floor, Mr. Justice Riley.

'Good evening, sir', he said, smothering his surprise.
'Your presence seems to complete the company. We're
just about to go into another room.'

At that moment the sounds of more cars coming to
violent halts in the road outside could be heard and heavy
feet pounded up the stairs. It was with some relief that
Manton welcomed his reinforcements. As his small band
of dazed suspects filed out of the room, the photographer
and fingerprint expert entered and quickly got down to work.

'Dr. Dill will be here in a few minutes, sir', called out
Talper from the clerks' office where he was still busily
telephoning.

Manton turned to a young detective officer who had just
arrived.

'Take these five ladies and gentlemen into that room
down the passage, but see that they don't speak with each
other.' In a whispered aside, he added, 'The half-pint
size one is a High Court judge. Treat him the same as the
rest, but don't put a match too close to him as he's liable
to go off. I'll join you in a moment.' Turning back into
Christopher's room, he closed the door behind him.

'Messy job', said the photographer laconically as he knelt over Maureen and took a close-up of her shattered skull.

'I want the whole place done for fingerprints, George', said Manton, addressing the officer who was casting an expert eye along the surface of the desk. 'Especially this desk, the drawers and telephone.'

'Looks like the poker was the weapon all right, sir. I'll take that back to the Yard with me; it'll need extra careful handling. Seems to have blood all over it.'

'What about all this paper and stuff on the floor, sir?' chimed in the photographer. 'I suppose I'd better take a picture or two of that?'

'Most certainly. Someone obviously did a rush job on these drawers looking for something. Presumably the murderer.'

Indeed the whole floor in the area of the desk and Maureen's body was littered with documents and papers and gave a generally blitzed appearance.

'Or it might have been the dead girl who was caught in the act by the murderer', said the fingerprint officer.

'Could be. O.K., lads, I'll go and join our friends next door. Let me know at once if you find anything of interest.'

Manton found his small band of suspects engulfed in a deep silence which none of them showed any inclination to break. In the circumstances he couldn't help thinking that the expression of the young officer whom he had posted guard over them was unnecessarily forbidding. He was surprised to observe that even the judge appeared to have relapsed into a state of submission, though he noticed that he had seated himself in the one and only comfortable chair, all the others being ranged round the walls on hard ones.

His return to their presence appeared to evoke very little

outward reaction, though his sixth sense reported a quickening tension behind the façade of silence. He turned towards Robin who was sitting between the two women agitatedly twining a forelock of his hair.

'I take it, Mr. King-Selman, that you are prepared to assist me by answering questions,' he began, at the same time casting a wary glance at the judge, 'but I must warn you that you're not obliged to say anything unless you so wish . . .'

'My son won't say anything without a solicitor being present', interposed Celia. 'It would be most unfair to question him now, and anyway what right . . .'

'I am conducting this inquiry, madam, and I would be glad if you would refrain from interfering, otherwise I shall have to ask you to leave the room. Now, Mr. King-Selman, are you ready to help?'

'Yes.'

'Darling, don't answer . . .'

'Please, Mummy, I know what I'm doing', said Robin, suddenly sitting up, his eyes large and brightly alert behind his spectacles.

'What time did you get here?' asked Manton.

'Just before half past eight.'

'Why did you come?'

'Maureen – er – that is, Miss Fox, phoned me about half an hour before and asked me to come at once. She said that something very important to do with my stepfather's death had just come to light.'

None of the officers present in the room could fail to notice the exchange of looks which this remark occasioned. Looking quickly from one to the other, Manton said, 'Am I right in thinking that each of you came in answer to a similar summons? Lady Riley?'

'Yes.'

'Mr. King-Selman?'

'Correct', replied Marcus primly.

'Mrs. Henham?' Celia nodded.

'Sir Gethin?'

'I think it would be of assistance to you if I were to explain', began the judge, when Manton broke in sharply.

'If you please, sir, just answer the question.'

'I received a similar telephone summons', said the judge frigidly.

'I see.' Turning back to Robin, Manton went on, 'How did you get here?'

'By taxi.'

'To the door?'

'No, it dropped me at the Law Courts.'

'And what did you find on your arrival here? Be very careful how you answer, Mr. King-Selman.'

'I came up the stairs and knocked on the outer door, but there was no answer. I could see a light shining beneath, so after knocking again, I tried the handle and found it wasn't locked. The hall was in darkness and I saw that the light was coming from my stepfather's room.'

'Was the door to it open?'

'Half-open.' Robin took a deep breath and in an over-casual tone continued, 'I went over and peered in and there was Maureen lying dead on the floor.'

'Yes?'

'I went over to her and could see that she was dead.'

'Did you touch her?'

'I just put my hand over her heart.' At this point Robin took another deep breath and steadied himself like an aeroplane coming in to land. 'I was absolutely horrified and dazed and I suppose I must have picked up the poker, because the next thing I knew was that Lady Riley was in the room and I had it in my hand.'

'But can you explain why you picked it up?'

'No, it must have been some reflex action.' Robin

139

stood up and throwing out his hands in a theatrical gesture added, 'I have told you the truth, but I suppose you're now going to arrest me.'

For a moment Manton eyed him with detachment and then said quietly, 'Sit down, Mr. King-Selman.' Turning to Helen he said, 'And do you confirm all that so far as it affects you, Lady Riley?'

'Yes. You see, I was up in my bedroom when Miss Fox telephoned my husband and I listened to the conversation on the extension. We heard Miss Fox suddenly cry out; obviously the murderer was attacking her at that moment, and after a while everything went silent. As soon as my husband left I got dressed and came along too, I was so worried.' She paused and looked expectantly at Manton. 'Well, you know the rest. I got a taxi which dropped me at the end of Templar's Passage and when I arrived here, I found Robin just as he has described. But of course he didn't do it.'

'No?'

'He'd hardly stand over her like that if he had.'

'It often happens that way in real life you know', Manton said dryly. 'And Mr. Marcus King-Selman, Mrs. Henham and your husband all arrived after you did, is that right, Lady Riley?'

'Yes.'

'Though your husband left the house before you did?'

'Yes', said Helen slowly, looking toward the judge. His only response was to bestow coldly dispassionate stares on both her and Manton.

'And then you arrived, Mr. King-Selman, followed shortly after by Mrs. Henham?'

'Correct', said Marcus with military brevity.

'Where was Lady Riley when you got here?'

'On the phone in the clerks' room.'

'And your son?'

'Standing by the body – but *not* holding the poker.'

'And you had received an urgent call from Miss Fox to come here?'

'Correct.'

'Where were you when she phoned?'

'At my hotel.'

'Which is?'

'The Astoria Palace in the Strand.'

'Quite close?' Marcus shrugged his shoulders disdainfully. 'What time did you receive the call?'

'Just before eight.'

'But you didn't arrive till half past?'

'Because she told me to come in half an hour's time.'

'Miss Fox said that?'

'Yes.'

Manton now turned his attention to Celia. 'And you also came here in answer to a telephone summons, Mrs. Henham?'

'No.'

'But you told me earlier . . .'

'I know,' she cut in, 'but it didn't happen that way.'

'How did you then come to be here?'

'I spoke to Miss Fox on the phone this morning and told her that I wanted to come to Chambers and go through my husband's personal effects. She said she had something she wished to discuss with me in private and could I come along about half past eight this evening. I agreed.'

'I see', Manton said thoughtfully. 'Where did you come from?'

'I went to a newsreel cinema in the Strand, and after that I had a snack at the Corner House and came on from there.'

'Were you alone at the cinema and Corner House?'

'Yes.'

'And how did you travel here?'

'I walked.'

'And you arrived for the first time just after Mr. Marcus King-Selman?'

'Yes', said Celia, and Manton detected a note of defiance in her voice.

Marcus had sat motionless throughout this exchange of question and answer with only his eyes darting from Manton to Celia, but he now suddenly spoke. 'That's a monstrous innuendo, officer: suggesting that Mrs. Henham had been here earlier.'

Manton took no notice of the interruption and still addressing Celia said, 'Did Miss Fox give you any idea what it was she wanted to talk to you about?'

'None.'

'None at all?'

'None.'

'But you gathered it was connected with your husband's death?'

'I didn't say so.'

'No, but did you?'

'Yes, I supposed it was to do with my husband, but not necessarily with his death.'

Manton looked across at the judge. 'Can you explain, sir, why, if you left your house before Lady Riley, you arrived here after her – in fact, after the police too?'

'For the very simple reason that I didn't come direct.'

'Where did you stop on the way?'

'I called in at my club.'

'For how long?'

'I am not in the habit, officer, of carrying a stop-watch and timing my every movement', he replied unpleasantly.

'And did the taxi wait for you at your club?'

'I've never said I was in a taxi.'

'How then did you travel, sir?'

142

'By taxi.'

The two men eyed each other with silent distaste. Uppermost in Manton's mind was the fervent hope that should his lordship's judicial career unfortunately turn out to have any future, it should never lead him into the criminal courts where police and prisoners would undoubtedly vie for his odium. At that moment the fingerprint officer came into the room and whispered to Sergeant Talper, who, after an intent study of the judge's feet, came over to Manton. There was another whispered confabulation and Manton then addressed the judge.

'If, as you say, sir, you only arrived here for the first time after everyone else, can you explain how you come to have traces of blood on the side of your left shoe?'

CHAPTER FIFTEEN

Four pairs of eyes switched to the judge's left foot. Only its owner disdained to do likewise. Instead he slowly took a tin of Umujubes from his pocket and, removing the lid, studied the contents as if they were of infinitely greater concern to him at that moment than anything else. He extracted one and put it in his mouth. It seemed an æon of time before he put the tin away again and looked up to meet Manton's gaze.

'Are you a scientific expert, officer?' he asked, and then immediately answered the question himself. 'You are not, of course; but by suggesting that I have blood on one of my shoes, you're setting yourself up as such. In fact, to employ a colloquialism, you are drawing a bow at a venture, though you must surely know what a hazardous pastime that can be.' His tone, which had been deceptively soft, now hardened. 'In this instance you will very soon discover how perilous it is to jump to such unwarrantable conclusions, at any rate where one of Her Majesty's judges is concerned.' Getting to his feet, he went on, 'I do not issue idle threats, officer, but I can assure you that you will pay dearly for your defamatory and impertinent suggestions. And now I'll be off.'

Before he could move, however, Manton took a couple of paces and barred his way.

'If you insist upon leaving now, sir, I can't of course prevent you – but you'll have to do so without your shoes.'

The battle was now truly joined and the spectators watched agog as Manton and Mr. Justice Riley stood facing one another: the C.I.D. man quiet, impersonal and in full command; the judge small and smouldering angrily with affronted dignity.

'Furthermore, sir, you are now apparently trying to remove the blood in full view of a lot of witnesses.' The judge had indeed been making surreptitious efforts to rub his shoe on the carpet by quietly turning over his ankle.

'How dare you! I'll have you flung out of the police force by tomorrow morning.'

'In the meantime I'll have your shoes, sir.' Manton turned to Talper. 'Sergeant, find Mr. Justice Riley some alternative footwear to get him home.'

'And if I refuse to remove my shoes?' the judge asked viciously.

'I'll phone the Commissioner, sir; tell him the facts and ask him to get in touch immediately with the Lord Chancellor and Home Secretary.'

That should finally call his bluff, Manton thought to himself, and indeed it did. Without a further word, Mr. Justice Riley sat down again and removed both his shoes, kicking them angrily away from him with a stockinged foot. The indignity of disclosing a large hole in one sock through which his big toe poked was aggravated by Sergeant Talper's return to the room with an ancient and shapeless pair of plimsolls.

'I'm afraid these are the best I can manage, sir', he said, handing them to Manton with the merest flicker of a wink.

Manton now found himself in something of a fix. The sum of his recent efforts had been to ask a lot of questions and dispossess a judge of his shoes. He had arrived at the scene of the crime within little more than half an hour of its commission and now had within touching distance five people, one of whom almost certainly was a double murderer. But which one? In the ordinary way he knew that he would be quite justified in arresting Robin and charging him with Maureen's murder, but while he didn't dismiss this as an ultimate possibility, there was something about it which completely confounded the few hunches he had cautiously formed. But what to do? He couldn't keep them sitting there all night in the vain hope that the murderer might suddenly break down and confess. And yet the prospect of allowing them to disperse was even worse, for with them might go vital clues and the last hope of ever solving the case. He felt like a man playing a difficult hand of bridge. If played correctly, victory was assured, but one false move and the initiative would pass irrevocably to his opponents.

The arrival of Dr. Dill gave him a welcome breathing space. Leaving Sergeant Talper to watch over his small submissive group, he went back to Christopher's room.

'Good evening, doctor.'

'Hello, Manton', replied Dr. Dill, throwing his raincoat on to a chair and undoing the buttons of his shirt cuffs. 'What's someone trying to do? Blot out the legal profession and its minions? Incidentally, all right for me to disturb things in here?'

'Yes; we've finished photographing and fingerprinting.'

Slipping on a pair of rubber gloves, Dr. Dill knelt down beside Maureen's body and, carefully avoiding the bloody mess by her head, made a quick but expert examination.

'That the weapon?' he asked, nodding at the poker.

'Almost certainly, I think.'

'What happened?'

'It seems she was in the act of telephoning Mr. Justice Riley when she was suddenly attacked. The judge and his wife both say they heard her groans and then the line went quiet, apart from some indeterminate noises which seem to be consistent with their having listened in to a murder being committed.'

'Mmm', said the doctor thoughtfully. 'It all fits. She was clearly attacked from behind, the great mass of the blows falling on the crown of her head. The poor girl must have been belaboured to death.'

'Any idea how many blows were struck?'

'I can't tell you with any accuracy before I do a full autopsy, but I should guess not fewer than half a dozen.'

'How severe?'

'Tell you definitely later, but again they must have been good hard cracks.'

'I suppose they could have been delivered by a woman?'

'Oh, yes, I should think so', said the doctor airily. 'You don't have to be all that muscular to crack someone's head open with a poker, particularly if you take them by surprise. You usually stun 'em with the first blow and then they're easy prey. But I'll answer all these questions for you when I've done the P.M. Got anyone lined up for it yet?'

For the next few minutes Manton told him the gist of his information about the crime. At the end Dr. Dill shook his head doubtfully.

'Not often you catch someone standing red-handed over the corpse and he doesn't turn out to be the right Johnnie. Isn't he the one who also dabbles in chemistry and keeps a handy supply of potassium cyanide?'

'Used to keep', replied Manton and explained.

'Very significant.'

'But what about the judge having blood on his shoe, when according to his story he only arrived at Chambers long after everyone else and then never came into this room? Dammit, that's significant if anything is', expostulated Manton. 'You see, he is the one person, who, on his own showing, has no excuse for blood being on him. Any of the others might reasonably talk themselves out of the difficulty, since they were all in this room when I arrived and they could have trodden in the mess unawares. But not the judge, unless . . . unless he's lying about the time of his arrival and that when he suddenly appeared in that doorway as we were about to leave the room, it was in fact his second appearance.'

'But you've no other reason, apart from the blood on his shoe, for thinking that, have you?' said Dr. Dill, more as a positive assertion than as a question.

'I'm not so sure about that', Manton replied. 'There's a further point. Despite the fact that he left his home some minutes before his wife did, he didn't arrive here till well after her.'

'But I thought he'd explained that.'

'Dropped in at his club, he said', observed Manton sceptically. 'We'll check that naturally, but on the face of it, it's scarcely a watertight alibi.'

'Well, I'd suspend your suspicions until you've established that the blood on his shoe is the same as the girl's. Coincidences do happen in your job and this could be one.'

'All I can say is that if it is, it'll be one hell of a coincidence. Slaughterhouse employees may often innocently get blood on their shoes; even pathologists, but not High Court judges.'

Dr. Dill gave Manton a shrewd smile and said, 'I'll be on my way. The sooner I get going, the sooner I may be able to help you resolve a few of your headaches.' He rolled down his shirt-sleeves and buttoned them up as he walked across to collect his raincoat. 'Have the body sent along to the mortuary straightaway, will you?

I don't want to be up half the night doing this job, especially since it looks like being a fairly short and simple one – unlike our friend the Q.C.' He crossed the hall to the front door talking as he went. 'What about Mrs. Henham, got any hooks on her yet?'

Manton made an expressive Gallic gesture denoting the indefinite. 'As you know, wives are always prime suspects when their husbands get murdered. And, of course, poison together with pearl-handled revolvers are regarded as favourite feminine weapons.'

After a final word at the front door, the two men parted and Manton returned with heavy tread to the room where Sergeant Talper was still mounting guard over one murderer and four innocents. Of that much he was certain beyond doubt, but as to which was the murderer, he had not a clue – or so he felt.

The scene which greeted him was outwardly little different from that when he had left the room fifteen minutes before, but the whole atmosphere had perceptibly changed. It was as if, like a band of conspirators, they now divined the hopeless impossibility of his position and knew that for the time being they were on top.

Robin had lit a pipe and was unconcernedly puffing away; Marcus was whispering to Celia; Helen appeared to be completely lost in not displeasing thoughts of her own; and the judge, hunched in his chair, wore an enigmatic expression which gave Manton no cause for joy. It was he, the judge, who was the first to speak.

'And how much longer, officer, are you proposing to hold us *incomunicado*? It is now ten minutes to ten and you have detained us for approximately one hour. I presume', he went on acidly, 'that you are not proposing to keep us here all night merely in the hope that one of our number will suddenly break down and make a dramatic confession of guilt.'

149

This was so close to the train of thought which Manton had been vaguely pursuing, that he actually felt himself blushing. He had in fact been trying to decide how much longer he could justifiably hold them when the chances of any further revelations seemed out of the question. Aloud he said, 'I would like you all to come along to Scotland Yard and make signed statements concerning your movements and arrival here this evening.'

'Are you speaking of statements under caution?' the judge asked unpleasantly.

'Not in your case at the moment, sir', replied Manton, declining to quail at the question or the tone in which it was asked. Besides which, he reckoned that he probably knew as much, if not more, about the Judges' Rules than any Divorce judge.

Leaving a junior officer in charge of Chambers, they trouped out and packed into the waiting cars, Sergeant Talper ostentatiously bearing Mr. Justice Riley's shoes before him like a votive offering.

Big Ben was chiming ten o'clock as the short cortège turned off the Embankment. The last light of an early spring day had faded and the air had a soft magical quality that each year brings leaping hope to even the gloomiest weather prophet. The street lights were reflected in the broad sweep of the river, as, heedless of the human crises enacted daily on its banks, it flowed with deep majestic detachment toward the sea.

It was, however, only Sergeant Talper who gave any thought to these intangibles. Although he had been a member of the Metropolitan police for twenty-four years and had lived in London for all that time, his heart still belonged to the west of England where he had been reared midst conditions of a perfect country life. Each spring still found his stolid exterior hiding a heart which ached for green fields adorned with banks of yellow primroses and crystal-clear water gurgling happily beside a winding lane.

'Would you take Mr. Robin King-Selman to your room, Sergeant, and get a statement from him', said Manton as they reached the corridor where their offices lay. 'Under caution', he added in an aside which the others couldn't hear.

He had decided that tact and propriety required him to tackle the judge himself and also to give him precedence of audience over the others. The interview, however, turned out to occupy singularly less time than he had reckoned. Mr. Justice Riley watched him in silence as he gathered paper and pen and when at last Manton indicated that he was ready to begin, there were several moments silence before the judge, speaking slowly and softly, said:

'If you think, officer, that I am now going to make a statement for you to take down in writing, you are much mistaken, for I have no intention of doing anything of the sort. Tomorrow morning I shall first of all report your high-handed conduct to the Home Secretary himself and at the same time I shall make it known that if a statement is required of me, I will dictate one and forward it to the Commissioner, but that I do not propose to submit myself to interviews by impudent police officers of subordinate rank.'

Without a word Manton got up and opened the door. Mr. Justice Riley also rose and moved toward it.

'Is there a car to take me home?' he asked.

Manton fought back the almost irresistible urge to tell him there was not and furthermore that he hoped he'd have to travel by public transport and endure ribald comments on his incongruously-shod feet and, if possible, something yet more physical and painful than that. He realized, however, that it would be quite fatal to give him any true cause for complaint and contented himself with looking meaningly at his plimsolled feet before instructing a passing officer to escort his lordship to the front entrance and arrange transport for him.

'Will you not wait for Lady Riley, sir?' he asked.

'No. If you haven't a car for her, she'll have to get a taxi. You may tell her that I've gone.'

Manton watched him as he paddled down the corridor, his eyes boring into the judge's retreating back. A murderer? If he was, one thing was certain and that was the monumental legal and constitutional furore which his arrest would create. He continued staring into space for some moments after Mr. Justice Riley had disappeared from view, then walked across to the room opposite and fetched Celia.

She took a very different stand and talked so much that Manton was immediately put on his guard, knowing from experience how easily the one tiny but vital false fact or omission can be concealed in a spate of true detail.

To Manton, the most significant features of her account were that Maureen had suggested the Chambers meeting because she, Maureen, had something important to discuss with Celia. This something could only have been connected with Christopher. Christopher alive? or Christopher dead? He thought almost certainly the latter, but what was it and why did it require such a mysterious tête-à-tête? Another significant feature about Celia's story was that only a deliberate effort could have made her movements prior to arriving at Chambers so impossible to check. She had been not only alone, but in places where an individual face would never be remembered. Why? asked Manton of himself as he wrote down her statement.

'Which of you suggested the time of eight-thirty?' he asked.

'I believe I did.'

'Did anyone know you were going to Chambers at that hour? Your son perhaps?'

'No,' said Celia quickly, 'I never told Robin I was going and he couldn't possibly have known.'

'Mr. King-Selman?'

'Yes, I think I did mention it to him', she replied, in a tone too casual for Manton not to notice.

With a sudden change of tack he said, 'It seems probable, Mrs. Henham, that the same person murdered both your husband and Miss Fox.'

'But of course', Celia replied, a shade petulantly.

'I also have a feeling that your manslaughter case is all bound up with the murders.' As he spoke, he saw her look away from him and for a moment she gave the haggard appearance of a distraught woman near the end of her tether.

'You think that I may be a murderess; is that it?' she asked with a faint tremor in her voice.

'You or someone close to you', replied Manton evenly. There was a pause.

'Did you know that Lady Riley was in the car with my husband at the time of the accident?' she suddenly asked, and then added bitterly, 'Oh, but of course, you're not yet persuaded that I wasn't the driver.'

'How do you know that Lady Riley was there?'

Celia looked up at him in surprise. 'I put two and two together and confirmed my suspicion.'

'I see.'

'You believe me?'

'You're trying to tell me that that gave Lady Riley a motive for murdering your husband: that he had threatened to implicate her in order to secure your acquittal and she killed him to prevent a scandal. That's it, isn't it?'

153

'Well, it all fits, though I very much doubt whether Helen acted alone.'

'You think the judge was in it too? But that's always been your view.'

'Believe me, Superintendent, both Helen and Gethin Riley are quite capable of committing murder to protect themselves.'

'A surprisingly large number of people are, Mrs. Henham.'

Another silence fell between them and Manton reflected with a patient sigh that the laboratory experts had promised to let him know definitely on the morrow how the poison had been administered to Christopher. The answer to that should help to eliminate a number of his suspects. Should, but would it? he pondered. Aloud he said, 'Was your husband carrying on with another woman, Mrs. Henham?'

'Why do you ask that?'

'Because I want to know the answer. Because it's obviously important that I should know the answer.'

'I have no positive knowledge of any such thing.'

'Suspicions?'

'Christopher and I were devoted to each other but we weren't jealously possessive lovers. You see, we were both gregarious by nature.'

'I have reason to believe that Miss Fox had some kind of infatuation for your husband.'

'I knew nothing about it', said Celia woodenly.

'What were his feelings toward Lady Riley?'

'It would be more to the point to ask what were her feelings toward him.'

'Well, what were they?'

'Helen Riley is a predatory bitch', she replied, with real spite in her voice.

For a space Manton became lost in thought, then, to

Celia's surprise, he got up and perfunctorily ushered her out of his room.

The strain of the last hour had made its mark on Helen. Her tiny features looked pinched and it was as if ten years had been suddenly added to her age.

'Your husband has gone home already, Lady Riley', Manton said by way of introduction.

'So I gathered. I heard you speaking to him in the corridor. Did he satisfy you as to how he came to have blood on his shoe?'

He looked at her curiously. 'No, he didn't wish to make a statement and . . . and so that was that.'

'I see.'

'Lady Riley,' he said slowly and with great deliberation, 'were you in Mr. Henham's car on the evening of the accident?'

'Celia's been telling you things.'

Manton ignored the question form in which the remark was made and asked her again.

'Were you?'

'I must have time to think', she said desperately.

'It's hardly a question which requires any thought to answer.'

'Yes, I was with him', she said breathlessly. 'Now let me think for a few moments.'

He watched her intently as she rhythmically swayed about on her chair as though keeping her body in time with unheard music. Her face was a study in deep concentration. At last she looked up at him.

'I think I'd better tell you the whole story, Superintendent', she said. 'That Tuesday or whenever it was – I seem to have lost all sense of time since Christopher's death – he and I met at Mr. Lawford's cocktail-party. I expect you've heard of him, he's a well-known solicitor. We both got a bit bored with it after a time and decided to slip away and go and have dinner together. When we got outside the house, Christopher discovered that his Bentley was blocked in by other cars so he took his wife's car. We went to Chez Clovis for dinner and then Christopher said he must go back to Chambers to pick up some papers. As we were leaving the restaurant, he slipped on the pavement outside and hurt his thumb. However we went to Chambers, got the papers and he was then going to drop me home. On our way back we had this accident.' She broke off and made the small appealing gesture of a child about to tell its father of yet another broken pane in the greenhouse. 'I know we ought to have stopped; I told Christopher so, but he said he'd hardly touched the cycle and he was sure no real harm had been done to either the man or his machine. He was worried, I think, about having to give our names if we stopped. You see, although we'd spent a perfectly innocent evening together, nobody knew we were in each other's company and he foresaw all sorts of . . . well, of complications.' She shrugged her shoulders graphically to indicate the contingencies which might have had to be met should their presence together have become generally known. 'Well, I think you know the rest. Christopher dropped me at home and then soon after he got back to his house, the police arrived and Celia met them at the door and told them that she'd been driving at the time. After all it was her car', she added, telescoping a whole process of thought. 'Christopher agreed to let her take the blame as at the time it seemed to be the best thing for everyone. Unfortunately there was this hideously unforeseen development: the man died of his injuries and Celia was charged with manslaughter and the whole thing got out of hand.' She paused and a moment later concluded, 'Now I've told you it all and I'm personally very glad to have got it off my chest.'

'Did you and Mr. Henham discuss the situation before his death?'

'Constantly. He was terribly upset about it.'

'And what decision did you reach about your future course of action?'

'He wanted to tell the authorities immediately and me to support him. But I suggested we should wait a little longer before doing anything so drastic.'

'Why?'

'Because I still thought that the case against Celia Henham might not go on and the longer he could hold out, the better.'

'For you?'

'For both of us', she replied immediately.

'You weren't trying to dissuade him from disclosing the truth for ever?'

'Heavens, no. I simply tried to reason with him. I pointed out that his wife had voluntarily taken this on herself and that she was able to do so with far fewer repercussions than he. After all, he was in the running for a judgeship and this could just about have killed his chances.'

'Instead it's killed him.'

'What a macabre thing to say, Superintendent.'

'Tell me, Lady Riley, how did Mr. Henham get on with your husband? I believe they'd known one another for a considerable number of years.'

'Ever since they were Bar students together.' She hesitated and then said, 'Gethin is not a person who makes friends easily.'

And that's a piece of masterly understatement, thought Manton, apart from which it doesn't answer my question. He asked two more on the same topic, but it became readily apparent that Helen was not prepared to discuss her husband's relations with the deceased man or anyone else.

'Reverting for a moment to the car accident,' he said quietly, 'there's one thing that rather puzzles me. Mr. Henham was a driver of long experience. How did it come about that he knocked into this cyclist?'

'He was finding it very difficult to steer properly because of his injured thumb. You see any pressure on it was giving him pain.'

'That's the only explanation for his erratic driving?'

'Yes. Oh, I know what's in your mind, Superintendent, but I can promise you he wasn't the slightest bit drunk.'

'I haven't suggested it, Lady Riley.'

'No, but I can read your thoughts quite clearly. After all, isn't it the first thing the police look for in motor accidents: and how right, though not in this instance.'

Manton's next question never got asked since at that moment a young officer burst into the room and whispered into his ear. When he had finished, Manton said, 'Tell him I'll come now.' Turning to Helen he went on, 'That's all for the moment, Lady Riley. I'll arrange for a car to take you home.'

'I hope I have been of some assistance to you, Superintendent.'

'You have indeed, madam,' he replied and beneath his breath added, 'much more so than you probably realize or even intended.' Bidding her good night he hurried along to the room where Sergeant Talper was taking a statement from Marcus. On entering, he found Talper sitting back in his chair with his hands clasped across his stomach and eyeing Marcus with what might be described as judicial suspicion. For his part Marcus had the air of a Colonel kept unavoidably waiting on parade.

'Ah', said Talper as Manton entered. 'Now, Mr. King-Selman, would you kindly repeat to Superintendent Manton what you've just told me.'

Marcus cleared his throat and fixing Manton with a steady gaze said, 'I arrived at Henham's Chambers this evening just before half past eight. There was no one there except for Miss Fox, so rather than hang about I went to get some cigarettes. When I got back about ten minutes later, I found that Robin, Lady Riley and Mrs. Henham had arrived and Miss Fox was dead.'

'I don't follow. . . .'

Marcus impatiently brushed aside Manton's interruption and concluded, 'Ten minutes earlier she had been alive and perfectly well.'

CHAPTER SIXTEEN

THIS revelation was so totally unexpected that it was several moments before Manton spoke. Even when he did he was not certain that his mind had grasped the full import of what Marcus had just said.

'Where was she and what was she doing when you first got there?' he asked at last.

'She was in the room where you saw her body and appeared to be going through the drawers of Henham's desk.'

'Did you speak to her?'

'I just told her that I'd be back again in a few minutes.'

'How did she appear? Was she at all excited or out of the ordinary in any way?'

'Not that I noticed.'

'Did she say anything to you?'

'She simply said "all right" when I told her I'd be back in a few minutes.'

Manton frowned. The whole story had a most peculiar ring about it and he was far from satisfied that he had been told the truth.

'Did you see or hear anyone in the vicinity of Chambers when you left to buy your cigarettes?'

'Nobody I knew.'

'Anyone at all?'

'Not that I can remember.'

'Mr. King-Selman, the Temple is fairly deserted after

business hours', Manton said severely. 'Did you or did you not see anyone in the neighbourhood of Chambers?'

'No, I did not', replied Marcus sharply.

'Is there any way I can check your story?'

Marcus flushed angrily at the tone of doubt and incredulity in Manton's voice.

'As a matter of fact there is', he said defiantly. 'I threw an empty cigarette packet into the waste-paper basket beside Henham's desk and you should find it there if you look.'

'What sort of cigarette packet?'

'A packet of twenty De Heide's Southern Rhodesian Special filtered. Not Players or Gold Flake you see, officer', he added, faintly jeering. 'I've yet to meet anyone else in this country who smokes De Heide's.'

'That's all very well,' replied Manton tartly, 'but how do I know you didn't drop it in the waste-paper basket on your return to Chambers?'

'As I've told you, when I got back, my son, Lady Riley and Mrs. Henham were already in the room. At least one of them would be sure to remember if I'd thrown anything into the waste-paper basket. Ask them. Apart from which it was hardly the time to perform such a trivial act.'

'It's not absolute proof of your story by any means', said Manton doubtfully.

'I should have thought, officer, that with all your experience you would be far more suspicious of so-called absolute proof than of something reasonably proved but not mathematically certain.'

The truth of this comment struck home and Manton silently acknowledged the validity of the argument. A short while later, Marcus, the last to leave, was on his way out.

161

The next morning at five past ten, Manton stepped into the Commissioner's office. The A.C.C. was already there and no time was lost in preliminaries.

When Manton had finished his narrative of the previous evening's events, a thoughtful silence ensued which he, himself, was the first to break.

'I've just come from the laboratory, sir. They say that the blood on the instep of the judge's shoe is of the same group as the dead girl's and identical to it in every way. They've also done a lot of experimenting with Umujubes and Capstick's Cough Capsules, trying to impregnate them with potassium cyanide and so forth, and have reached the conclusion that the poison must have been administered in a capsule. They've failed to find any satisfactory way of loading an Umujube and say that it would have been next to impossible to do so. On the other hand they point out that a capsule is the ideal method of introducing poison into someone's system.'

'That's all very fine,' said the Commissioner energetically, 'but it poses more questions than it answers. Anyway how do the lab. people account for the fact that Henham collapsed immediately after popping an Umujube into his mouth? It's too much of a coincidence that a few seconds before he had swallowed a poisoned capsule which took effect at that precise moment.'

'It could be that he never put an Umujube into his mouth at all', said the A.C.C.

'Well, we know he put something in and that he died almost at once. Remember he hardly had time to take his hand away from his mouth before he collapsed, and we know these capsules take two or three minutes to melt in the stomach and release their contents. Therefore I still put my money on its having been an Umujube.' He turned to Manton. 'Anyway now you know the lab.

findings you'd better go into the medical detail of it much closer with the lab. Director and Dr. Dill.'

Manton nodded. 'I will, sir.'

'Have you been down to Henham's country cottage yet?'

'No, sir; but I'm going to.'

'I think you should. You might learn something useful; pick up some bit of background.'

'Yes, sir; also I want to take possession of the tin of potassium cyanide which is in the garden shed down there. It seems almost certain that it was the original source of supply to the murderer. That is either direct or via young King-Selman's laboratory.' He read the Commissioner's thoughts and added, 'I haven't bothered too much about it to date, sir, since I believed it to be a less important aspect of the case than others which have been occupying my time here in town. After all, both the Henhams and the Rileys knew it was there, their finger-prints on the tin could be easily explained and I doubt whether it will tell us anything we don't already know.'

'All the same I think you should get hold of the stuff without delay', said the Commissioner briskly but not unkindly.

'I will, sir. To-day.'

'Well, let's see where we've got to', said the Commissioner, leaning back in his chair and caressing his moustache. 'Henham was poisoned by potassium cyanide, which was administered to him by means of an Umujube or a capsule. If it was a capsule, are we agreed that the probability is there was an exchange of tubes: i.e. that Henham was slipped a whole tube which looked perfectly ordinary, but which in fact contained the poisoned capsule? I can't personally see that the murderer would carry about one loose poisoned capsule hoping for an opportunity to plant it amongst Henham's own supply, for that would be too much like trying to plant a pineapple in a window-box without attracting attention.'

Both the A.C.C. and Manton nodded sagely and the Commissioner continued with his reconstruction of the crime, but contrived to say nothing which Manton and Talper hadn't already discussed together. After reviewing the five suspects' opportunities for committing the two murders, he turned to their motives. 'Of course no one could have had a stronger one than Mrs. Henham and it's difficult to conceive of any English husband behaving with less chivalry and a greater degree of pusillanimity than Henham. And for all we know, he never really had the slightest intention of coming clean.'

'Except, sir,' broke in Manton, 'that he got me along to his house to ask my advice and I'm sure his wife didn't know anything at all about my visit.'

'Exactly. And what was your reaction to his story? You didn't believe it. He knew you wouldn't. He would have been horrified and completely put out of countenance if you had. No one was likely to believe such a story.'

'And yet it was a true one', persisted Manton.

'I agree; but should we ever have been persuaded of that without his death?'

'But surely, sir, if Mrs. Henham murdered her husband, she was destroying her best chances of acquittal. With him alive, there was always hope that things would get put right, but once he was dead, no one was likely to believe her if she suddenly said he was driving the car when the accident occurred. You've got to remember she didn't know her husband had spoken to me nor did she know for certain at the time of her husband's murder that Lady Riley had also been in the car.'

'Well, all I can say,' retorted the Commissioner, 'is, that if I had behaved toward my wife as Henham did toward his, she would be fully entitled to murder me.'

The A.C.C. raised one mildly quizzical eyebrow and gave Manton a covert glance of amusement, the Commissioner's wife being a formidable Amazon who in her day had been a crack rifle shot. This attainment together with her physique was a not infrequent source of funny stories among the lower echelons of the Metropolitan police.

'As for her son and ex-husband,' he went on, 'they each have the same motive, namely to avenge the wrong done to the woman they love by a man they certainly don't. Does that sum it up fairly?' he asked, looking from Manton to the A.C.C.

'Isn't the avenging motive a little outmoded in this day and age?' asked the A.C.C. gently. 'Does anyone nowadays really kill another in order to vindicate the position of a third person? Personally I should very much doubt it and I wouldn't therefore consider it much of a motive so far as the younger King-Selman is concerned. But the elder one is quite a different kettle of fish. Obviously he's never lost his love for his ex-wife and I could easily see him murdering Henham from a blend of motives in which jealousy predominated and your suggested one, sir, was maybe the final weight which tilted the scales.'

The Commissioner sailed on again as soon as the A.C.C. stopped speaking. 'We mustn't forget of course that once we have enough evidence to prefer a charge, motives lose all their relevance. Happily, we don't yet in this country have to prove a motive in criminal cases and they're only helpful in getting one on to the right trail, eh Manton?'

'True, sir, but many a murderer has escaped conviction because the Crown couldn't pin a motive on him. Show a jury it was done from gain or greed or jealousy or lust and you make their task a much easier one.'

'Just what I've always said', the Commissioner replied without hesitation or truth. 'However, let's finish our survey of motives. Against Lady Riley we can prove a really strong one: to silence the man who might otherwise involve her in a scandal – and, mind you, it had all the makings of a really nasty scandal for a judge's wife. As for the judge himself, he can be tied up with his wife.'

Manton listened fascinated by the way motives were enthusiastically dealt round like a pack of cards. There was something almost naïve about some of the Commissioner's thought processes or so it seemed to Manton. For example, his recently expounded view on Helen Riley's motive. From what she had told Manton, she could never have felt certain, if she *were* the murderess, that she hadn't acted too late and that Christopher hadn't already implicated her – as, in fact, he must have done or how else could Celia have known and later taxed her with it. A poisoned pill indicated careful preparation and time to act which Helen could never have allowed herself, if the motive postulated for her by the Commissioner was a valid one.

The Commissioner was speaking again. 'Finally, let us consider last night's murder of Maureen Fox. What do we know – or think we know about that?' There was no doubt that he was savouring to the full his role of summer-up, as, wearing his most judicial expression, he went on, 'Between half past seven and eight, three people received excited telephone calls from the murdered girl asking them to go immediately to Chambers to hear of some dramatic development concerning Henham's death. Those three were the two King-Selmans and Sir Gethin Riley. Mrs. Henham was due to arrive there at eight-thirty as a result of an arrangement made between herself and the murdered girl earlier in the day. Lady Riley didn't receive a call herself but listened in on an extension while Miss Fox was speaking to her husband.' He paused for dramatic effect and fixing his small audience with a gimlet eye, continued, 'The first to answer the summons and arrive at Chambers was King-Selman senior. He arrived just before half past eight, having had no more than a ten-minute walk from his hotel. And what does he tell us? That Miss Fox was then alive and well, and apparently alone in Henham's room going through the drawers of his desk. And what does he do? He goes off to buy some cigarettes rather than wait for the others to come. That, despite the fact that he had only just come from his hotel and might have been expected to have remedied the deficiency before setting out. Anyway, that is what he tells us, and off he goes leaving Miss Fox rummaging in the drawers of the desk without, I think I may safely say, either propriety or right. Young King-Selman arrives next and he cannot at the most have been more than a very few minutes after his father had left. He finds Miss Fox lying dead on the floor with her battered head in a pool of blood. For no reason which he can adequately explain, he picks up the blood-stained poker with which she has obviously been done to death and mounts guard over her body, thus to be discovered by Lady Riley. While she is phoning for the police, Mrs. Henham arrives, followed by King-Selman senior on his return. Then minutes later after you've arrived on the scene, the judge turns up. Despite the fact that he had left his house some time before his wife, she had arrived at Chambers before him. And that isn't the only significant fact about his arrival.' There was another pause for effect, though both the A.C.C. and Manton knew well what was coming. 'Although he never in your presence entered Henham's room, let alone go near the body, blood of recent origin is found on the instep of his left shoe – blood which is similar to the dead girl's.' The Commissioner lent forward and clasped his hands together on top of his desk. 'Well, there it is and which of us can fail to doubt that one, at least, of those five has lied to us? And the damnable thing is,' he added in a tone of exasperation, 'that if you put against the name of each the opportunity and motive he or she had for committing either of the murders, it works out an almost exact deadheat.'

'Not quite, sir', said Manton quietly. The two senior men immediately turned and looked at him and he added quickly, 'But I hope you'll give me a little longer, sir, before you press for details.'

'Are you on to something?' they asked in unison.

Manton assumed a mildly deprecating expression. 'I've collected one or two substantial straws but I'm still a long way from manufacturing a brick.'

'Well, see you don't drop the damned thing', said the Commissioner tersely.

Two hours later, with Sergeant Talper at the wheel, the two Yard officers were driving down the long hill which leads into Henley. The greater part of the journey had been accomplished in silence, though from time to time Manton had tapped Talper's recollection for some fact or detail of conversation. The replies had been followed by further stretches of silence or by the oddly scrambled sound of Manton thinking aloud, both of which Talper knew better than to interrupt. He realized that Manton, sooner rather than later, would divulge his thoughts and he could already recognize signs which indicated progress following his superior officer's intense cerebration.

As the car reached the bottom of the hill, Manton

wound his window down to its fullest extent and putting his nose out like an enamoured retriever sniffed deeply.

'Beautiful spring air', he said contentedly. 'It should do your heart good to have a few hours in the country, Andy.'

'Country?' retorted Talper contemptuously. 'This is all suburbia.'

'Oh, nonsense', replied Manton, laughing. 'Just how far do you have to get from London before you consider yourself to be in the country?'

Talper carefully considered the question.

'West of a line between Oxford and Southampton', he said at last. Manton chuckled and Talper went on, 'These people who live round here are nearly all London workers. London is where they earn their bread and butter, save for most of them it's fillet steaks and asparagus. You can't call this real country, though I grant you it's quite pretty in its way.' This last grudging concession was made as the car crossed the bridge into the town and he glanced at the serenely beautiful view of the river to their right.

For the next fifteen minutes Manton was happy to sustain the argument which he had unwittingly provoked and which ultimately proved to be the cause of their missing the Henhams' cottage and of having to turn back.

When finally they did arrive, they parked the car in the lane outside and walked slowly round it peering in at the downstairs windows, all of which were hermetically sealed.

'It's certainly a very pleasant spot on a day like this', said Manton as they stood on the lawn at the back and surveyed the garden. 'I suppose that must be the Rileys' cottage', he went on, nodding his head in the direction of the large beech tree which half-shielded it from their view. 'Let's go across and take a look.' They did so and found it as deserted as the one they had just left.

'Like a couple of Marie Celestes', said Manton when they had completed their inspection.

'Did you expect otherwise?' asked Talper in some surprise.

'No, not really, I suppose', Manton replied dreamily. 'Now for a squint at the garden shed. That must be it over there.' They walked across to a small rectangular log-cabin type of shed and found the door latched but unlocked. Inside was the usual clutter of garden implements, new and ancient, four chipped and deformed crocquet balls and a shelf-load of bottles whose dust-encrusted condition would have denoted a rare and precious vintage if they had contained wine instead of turpentine, methylated spirits and other infrequently consumed fluids.

'Don't see anything that looks like a tin of potassium cyanide, do you, Andy?'

Sergeant Talper shook his head and grunted a negative. A further short search confirmed their finding – or rather lack of it. They had just emerged on to the lawn again when a belligerent shout took them from the rear.

'Hi, you. What'y'doing in that shed? I'll have police on t'you.'

'We are the police', replied Manton, walking across to the owner of the voice. It took more than this, however, to allay the old man's suspicions and Manton had to explain patiently why they had been trespassing.

''Course that wasp poison's still there', the old gardener replied with vigour when he had heard them out. He led the way back to the shed and entered. 'It was up on that there shelf, I knows it was. Now 'oo the blazes can have shifted it?' He pulled viciously at the lobe of his right ear as if it might release the answer. Then, rather like a terrier burrowing for a rat, he moved every movable article in the shed in an energetic search for the missing tin of poison. But at the end it was still missing.

'Has any member of either of the families been down here since Mr. Henham's death?' Manton asked, as they stood outside the shed in the warm sunshine.

'No, none of 'em's been near the place.' He paused and had another pull at his ear. 'That is, *I* tain't seen any of 'em here.' He paused again. 'I meantersay, none of 'em tain't been down here official like.' He looked at Manton with eyes which managed to be rheumy and cunning at the same time.

'What do you mean to say?' asked Manton, deliberately jingling the loose change in his pocket.

'Well, I did hear something in village last evening but I don't pay attention to everything what's said to me.'

That Manton could readily believe. 'What did you hear?' he asked, at the same time clinking two half-crowns in the old man's view.

'That judge'd been here.'

'When?'

'Last Wednesday evening.'

'Who saw him?'

The old man eyed the coins greedily before replying.

'Emily saw him. She's the one what comes in and gets the places ready for them at week-ends. She was sure it was the judge she saw driving through about seven o'clock. He was coming from the direction of the cottage and wasn't half going a pace, she said. It was that that made her look at the car and then she see'd him. But what's so funny is the judge he normally drives so slow and careful. He never was one for speed.'

He finished his peroration well out of breath and it seemed probable that he had never before succumbed to such a flight of oratory. The two half-crowns changed hands without a word and Manton nodded his head in silent thought.

'Not a word of this to anyone', he said at last. 'Understand?'

It was the old man's turn to nod his head, though Manton reckoned they'd be lucky to get clear of the village before news of their visit was being promulgated.

They had started their journey back to town before either of them spoke again and then Sergeant Talper said, 'Looks as though it was the judge who spirited the tin of poison away.'

'I agree, Andy.'

'Wonder where he's hidden it?'

'Either in a deep hole in the garden or at the bottom of the river, I should say at a guess', replied Manton, in a tone he might have used to forecast the next day's weather. Talper shot him a sideways glance of surprise but instead of elucidating his answer, Manton sat back in silent thought, his mind obviously off on another tack. After a space he suddenly said, 'Let's hear your views on the two murders, Andy.'

Though the invitation was almost limitless in its range, Talper was ready for it.

'My view is that Mr. Henham was murdered by means of a poisoned capsule which must have been administered to him by either his wife or one of the two King-Selmans. I don't believe that he could have been poisoned by an Umujube and that lets out the judge and his wife.'

'Just before you go any further, how do you then account for the deceased's immediate collapse when we know that the capsules take some time to have effect, and also for the fact that traces of Umujubes were found in his body?'

'The capsules don't *have* to be swallowed, do they? I'm prepared to bet that when the judge urged Mr.

Henham to take an Umujube, he in fact put one of his own capsules into his mouth and then bit it. Remember, sir, he was having a rough time with that cough of his and therefore what more likely than that he should bite the thing in order to get a quicker effect? As for the other point, he probably did suck an Umujube some time within an hour or so of dying – in fact he must have done if the doctor says so, *but* it wasn't one of them he put in his mouth immediately prior to his collapse and death.'

'I entirely agree', said Manton.

'You do?' Sergeant Talper sounded almost suspicious of Manton's ready accord.

'Yes, certainly I do. I'm sure that's how it happened; I've thought so for some time. And you deduce that it must have been given to him by one of the three people you mention?'

'Yes. I think the Rileys are eliminated as we haven't a scrap of evidence that either of them could have tampered with the capsules. In any event this case has all along seemed to me to bear the hallmarks of a family affair.'

'What order of precedence do you put them in?'

For a time the question went unanswered as Talper concentrated his energies on overtaking a convoy of army lorries, but once they were on a clear stretch of road again, he said, 'I think it probable that King-Selman senior was the actual murderer: that is that it was he who devised the plan and was responsible for the major part of its execution. But I'm also fairly satisfied that his son must have been in it to some degree. Possibly he only had guilty knowledge; but that there was some sort of collusion between them, I feel certain.'

'For example, that Master Robin manufactured the poisoned capsule to the order of his father?'

Talper nodded enthusiastically. 'Yes. Who better able

than he to fix it? He had both materials and know-how ready to hand.'

'And what do you reckon was their motive?'

'The obvious one. I think King-Selman senior had always hated Henham for stealing his wife and that the final car episode was like pouring oil on to the smouldering embers of a fire. I wouldn't be surprised to learn that King-Selman had in fact threatened Henham about it. It's the sort of way he'd react.'

'But is poison the weapon of an angry, jealous, Empire-building type like King-Selman?'

'I don't see why not', replied Talper defensively. 'After all, once he'd resisted the impulse to fell Henham in the heat of the moment, he had all the time in the world to prepare the murder. Furthermore,' he went on with growing assurance, 'it seems to me that poison is very much the choice of someone in whose heart black jealousy has been smouldering for a number of years.'

Though Manton was refraining from commenting on Talper's theories, he was carefully chewing on each and then accepting, assimilating or discarding according to flavour.

'And what about the second murder?' he asked.

'Obviously done by the same person', said Talper without hesitation. 'On his own admission, King-Selman senior was the first to arrive at Chambers. I don't doubt that he's also telling the truth when he says that Miss Fox was alive when he got there. But I'm equally certain that she was dead when he left a few moments later. It was such an easy thing to do. Kill her and depart, and then return cloaked in shining innocence.'

'You're full of poetic touches this afternoon, Andy. Black jealousy and cloaks of shining innocence. You'll be composing your evidence in blank verse next. The Christopher Fry of the witness-box, they'll call you.

But to be serious, why, if you're right about Marcus King-Selman, should he ever admit to having been there earlier? Why not let it be thought that his return was in fact his first arrival?'

'I've thought of that, sir, and the explanation which comes to my mind is that for some reason he must have thought that his first visit could be discovered and therefore it was better to explain it away in advance rather than lie about it and be caught out.'

Manton looked dubious. 'I have no doubt we should have found it out by the cigarette packet he left in the waste-paper basket. But that was a clue he very carefully dropped himself. Why?'

'Because by the time he arrived at Chambers, he knew he'd been seen or had given himself away in some other manner.'

'Mmm, that's feasible. But what about young King-Selman who is found standing over the body, holding the bloody poker?'

'Either the innocent explanation he's given or part of a collusive scheme between him and his father to complicate the issue', Talper replied steadily.

'And what's your explanation for the blood on the judge's shoe?'

'That could have happened this way. Miss Fox is murdered as she is telephoning the judge. Spurred on by his wife, he sets out immediately for Chambers and arrives to find her dead. He suddenly realizes what a very awkward situation it is. I mean, he, a High Court judge, embroiled in a murder and being required to explain a whole lot of pertinent things. So what does he do but slip away and turn up again later when everyone else has arrived, pretending that he has only just come. Of course he doesn't know that on his previous visit he'd picked up some of the dead girl's blood.'

'Why did he come back at all in those circumstances? Why not go quietly back home?'

'Because his wife knew he'd set out for Chambers and it would be very difficult to explain satisfactorily why he'd never arrived there.' Talper gave Manton a quick glance. 'Does that seem a tenable theory to you, sir?'

'Yes, I think it's perfectly tenable. Indeed it's one I've been pondering myself.' He assembled his thoughts before going on, 'So you think that Marcus King-Selman arrived first, murdered Maureen and hopped off quickly again. Then the judge arrived, stood in the blood, and also decided to skip out quietly, though for different reasons. Next comes young Robin, followed by Lady Riley and Mrs. Henham. Then King-Selman senior comes back and finally we have the return of the judge. That it?'

'That's it, sir, and it seems to me that all the pieces fit perfectly. Everything points to King-Selman senior, with or without son, being a double murderer.'

He waited for Manton's approving comment, but after a thoughtful interval, the latter merely continued the interrogation.

'And what about the state of disorder in Henham's room? And you haven't yet suggested any motive for Maureen's murder.'

Sergeant Talper sighed, swerved to avoid an erratic cyclist and bent his mind to these further matters.

'Obviously someone was looking for something, presumably that recorded note which we think Mr. Henham probably made about matters connected with his death. Certainly all our suspects knew he had the habit of doing that and it's a fairly safe bet that if such a record does exist, it'll provide a clue to the murders. Hence the murderer's anxiety to find it.'

'You don't think it might have been Maureen herself

who was looking for it and who was caught in the act by the murderer?'

'It could have been that way, but I doubt it. Too much of a coincidence that she happened to be making a search in Mr. Henham's desk just as the murderer walked in.'

'Except that they had all been summoned by her to arrive there about half-past eight.'

'Yes, and doesn't that still further detract from the theory?'

'Mmm', said Manton weightily. 'I think you're probably right. The state of disorder implies that the murderer was in a hurry, and the damaged condition of the records that he or she had not time to find one particular record, so concentrated on destroying them all.'

'Which means that the murderer can't know whether or not he's been successful in obliterating his trail.'

'Exactly; and I'm sure he hasn't.'

'Oh?' said Talper, clearly surprised at so positive an assertion.

'No, because if it's what I think it is, Henham wouldn't have been likely to have kept it in Chambers.'

'Oh', Talper replied in a disappointed tone. He waited for further elucidation but none forthcame, Manton stating simply that he now had more than a good idea who the murderer was but it was all a question of finding evidence to prove it, and the sooner they got back to the Yard the better.

Although they had been out only a matter of four hours, Manton's desk in his absence had become piled high with reports, files, memoranda, circulars, one sawn-off shotgun and a thousand pounds in forged five-pound notes. With a groan he pushed it all aside like a snow-plough clearing an airfield and brought out from a drawer the rapidly growing file relating to his current inquiry.

Hardly had he opened it when Sergeant Talper joined him and dropped a small red-covered exercise book on to the desk.

'Maureen Fox's diary', he said laconically. 'Mrs. Fox handed it to Sergeant Minto when he was making some routine inquiries at the house this morning.'

Manton's eyes lit up with interest.

'So she kept a diary, did she?' he said as he flicked the pages. Then turning to the first page, he read, while Talper looked over his shoulder, 'Thursday, January 1st. Mr. Henham v. busy all day. No reference to yesterday evening!!! Mr. Exley was very stuffy as Mrs. E. had made him sit up and see the New Year in. Left Mr. H. still working in Chambers at 7. He insisted that I didn't stay on. What a wonderfully understanding person he is.'

'Interesting, and I wonder what happened "yesterday evening"', Manton said with obvious relish. 'Let's have a look a bit further on.' He flipped over the pages.

'Wednesday, April 8th', he read. 'C. in Court all day before that horrid, beastly Justice Riley.' He paused and commented, 'You'll note, Andy, that between January and April, "Mr. H." has become "C"'. He read on, 'This evening C. went to Mr. L.'s cocktail-party. Godfrey Luce was to be there. C. didn't want to go. He looked tired and I longed to be able to help him. And then a few hours later . . . Even now I don't know how I'm able to write it all down, except that it helps. But it's almost as if the hand writing these words is the hand of someone else, that of someone whose heart isn't jumping around like mine. But why did he have to do it where I might see: why give his wife loving embraces in Temple Row? It was almost as if he wanted me to see and be hurt. As soon as I stepped out of Chambers and saw her car parked up the road, I suspected something – at least I now know that I did. I can remember thinking that the radiator grille was sneering at me as I crossed over to the far side. And well it might have been for all that was going on inside. How my heart withered as I looked and saw. It was lucky I had crossed the road or I might have seized open the door and pulled C. out of her arms on to the pavement. All the way home in the bus I could see nothing else – only C. locked in his wife's embrace. I've tried to tell myself not to mind so much, but what's the good – and now at last I can confide in my diary.'

It continued in similar disjointed vein for another three pages and when they finally reached the end, Manton said quietly, 'Poor girl, she was completely infatuated with him.'

'But surely it wasn't his wife in the car with him that evening?' said Talper, puzzled.

'No, it was Lady Riley. Though probably it's just as well Maureen didn't know that or her upset would have been incomparably worse than it was.'

'I don't follow this. Why should she think it was Mrs. Henham if in fact it was Lady Riley?'

'I suppose seeing Mrs. Henham's car made her jump to the conclusion that the woman inside it was Mrs. Henham. After all, you don't see a great deal of anyone who is locked in an embrace. Their faces are hidden and, anyway, this was all going on inside a car; it must have been dark or almost so and she was on the opposite side of the road.'

Sergeant Talper took a deep breath. 'Then if it was Lady Riley who was behaving like this, we surely have the reason why she was so anxious for Mr. Henham not to disclose her presence in the car.'

'I don't see that', Manton said.

'Well if it had come out that —'

'But why should it have come out?' he broke in. 'She could quite well admit to being in the car without to bestowing her favours on another woman's husband.'

Talper scratched his head. 'But it's significant that we've only discovered it now. It must be significant', he added, almost pleadingly.

'You mean, of course, that it provides a motive for Lady Riley having murdered Henham?'

'Yes, and for her husband if he knew.'

'And for Mrs. Henham if *she* knew: not to mention Maureen who didn't know', said Manton in a faintly bantering tone. 'But you've already ruled out Sir Gethin and Lady Riley; you decided they had no opportunity and you can't just rope them in again as suspects simply because you've discovered they had rather better motives than you previously thought.'

'But do you mean that you don't regard it as significant our learning about Mr. Henham and Lady Riley carrying on this way?'

'It's certainly interesting', Manton conceded. 'But let's read on a little further.' He turned another page. 'Thursday, April 9th. When Mr. H. first sent for me this morning, I could hardly bring myself to enter his room.'

'Back to "Mr. H." again after last night's crisis', Manton observed and read on: 'He acted as though nothing had happened. Of course I never let on that I had seen him. He thanked me very sweetly for staying late and typing the opinion for him. If only he knew what staying late had cost me. . . .'

He turned the pages again.

'Monday, April 20th. C. terribly upset about his wife's motoring case. Couldn't tell him it was her fault for driving like that. . . .'

'Wednesday, April 22nd. Attended Mrs. H.'s proceedings at West Central Court. Reported back to C.

in Chambers. He was terribly distressed, but at the same time there was something strange about him. Something I didn't understand and which he wouldn't let me share.'

'Thursday, April 23rd. C. still v. preoccupied about Mrs. H.'s case. I've tried to help him and he's very sweet but won't let me. If only he would.'

'Friday, April 24th. C. the same. To-day I stayed after everyone had left and went through his desk to see if I could find any record he has made about his thoughts and feelings. If I knew, I'm sure I could help him. I couldn't find anything though I'm certain he has dictated something into the machine about it. He must have hidden it somewhere special. Ought I to feel ashamed? I do and yet I only did it for his sake.'

'Now that is both interesting *and* significant', said Manton, breaking off for a moment. 'It confirms what I said to you on our way back to town just now. Hello, what's this?'

He read: 'Monday, April 27th. SACKED. My heart is too full – and if only I could be certain that C. isn't at the bottom of it. . . .'

'Tuesday, April 28th. It is C. I can tell by his manner. He's awkward and embarrassed when I'm in the room with him now . . .' And this was the last entry in the diary.

'Stops short the day before Henham's death', said Manton, turning over a page and thoughtfully gazing at the blank one which followed.

'This all requires a great deal of thought', Talper suddenly said. 'Let me think it out straight, sir, and I'll tell you why our discovery about Mr. Henham and Lady Riley is so significant.'

'Before you do that, Andy, sit down and I'll tell *you* who the murderer is.'

CHAPTER SEVENTEEN

MANTON popped his head round the door of the room which Sergeant Talper shared with three other officers of the same rank.

'I've spoken to the A.C. and he's sure he'll be able to get the Commissioner to agree. Have you phoned Mrs. Henham?'

'Yes. She's in and can see us if we go round now, sir. Mr. and Master King-Selman aren't expected back till just before dinner. I found that out from competition Doris.'

'And Lady Riley?'

'She's also at home.'

'The judge?'

'Out.'

'Good.'

As the car bearing Manton and Talper westwards through the evening traffic laboriously edged its way round Hyde Park Corner, Manton said:

'I must say when we drove down to Henley this morning, I never dreamt that the end of the day would find us planning the final moves to catch our quarry. It's often the way, though; the last bits of the puzzle all fall into place surprisingly quickly.'

'I wouldn't be too optimistic, sir. This could still turn out to be an unsolved case unless we can find evidence to support a charge. We may think we know who is guilty, but unless they alter the rules of evidence we may never be able to prove it.'

'We've got to get hold of that record', said Manton, deeply engrossed in his own thoughts.

'But that's not evidence either.'

'Oh, blast evidence for the moment. It's still the vital key which will confirm what we already know and what we safely surmise.'

'And if we don't find it?'

Manton paused thoughtfully for a space before answering.

'If we don't find it; if we've completely stepped off on the wrong foot . . .' The sentence drifted away unfinished. 'But we must be right. I know we're taking a helluva risk, but what else can we do?'

'What did the A.C. think?'

'He thought it was a justifiable risk. He's certain we're right and will back us up to the hilt. And if we are right, then there are no risks involved at all', he concluded with the mercurial cheerfulness of a schoolboy whose algebra problem has suddenly been solved.

Sergeant Talper refrained from comment and frowned heavily as their car narrowly missed being scraped by a weaving taxi.

Their call on Celia lasted exactly twenty minutes. At its outset Manton felt his courage almost desert him as fresh doubts began to assail him. But it was too late to turn back now: the plan was embarked upon and must be seen through to the end.

When Doris let them out, Manton was far too excited and preoccupied to listen to her denunciation of the fashion editor of a Sunday newspaper who had, it appeared, deliberately cheated her out of a pressure cooker by rejecting her choice of accessories to go with an evening gown of exiguous proportions and a thrilling new shade called Octopus Smudge.

'So far, so good', said Manton, rubbing his hands as the car headed toward the Rileys' house.

'I'm afraid King-Selman is bound to smell a rat', replied Talper, contributing one of his many doubts about the enterprise. A deep silence ensued. Manton knew that he was not happy about the position; he never was when any unorthodoxy was introduced into police procedure. This despite the fact that on several occasions it was only by such methods that they had achieved their end.

On arrival at the Rileys' house, the ageless, silent Hislop answered the door and showed them into the same room in which Manton had had his first chilling encounter with the judge. While they waited for Helen, they prowled about like a couple of visiting cats, taking in every detail of the room. Manton noticed that a scribbling pad beside the telephone had disappeared since his last visit and that a box of wooden spills had been moved from one end of the mantelpiece to the other. They conversed together in the subdued tones appropriate to Church.

When Helen came in, Talper was gazing fixedly out of the window and Manton was sitting on the arm of a chair, whistling softly to himself and recalling idly that it was the first time he ever had sat down in that room.

'Good afternoon, Superintendent', she said, with a pleasant smile. Sergeant Talper's presence she acknowledged with a mere nod. 'What can I do for you? Your colleague here wasn't very communicative when he phoned.'

'I want to enlist your aid, Lady Riley', Manton said, choosing his words with care. 'I have a plan which largely depends upon your co-operation.'

'A plan connected with your investigation into the murders, I take it?'

'That is correct.'

'Well, if you tell me what it is you want me to do, I'll tell you whether or not I'm able to help you.'

'I'm quite sure you can help me, Lady Riley.'

'Be that as it may, let me first hear the plan.'

'I'm very anxious,' he said slowly, 'to have an opportunity of making an undisturbed search of the Henhams' house. You understand, of course, that what I now say is entirely between these walls and that even should you decline to do what I ask, you're not to breathe a word of it to anyone?'

'I can assure you that I'm quite used to keeping secrets, Superintendent – much greater ones than this in fact – so go ahead.' She lightly patted her trim little head as she spoke. Not a hair was out of place and her eyes were sparkling with anticipation. 'What are you hoping to find?' she asked and when Manton didn't immediately reply, she went on in a tone used for humouring children, 'But there's no need for you to answer. It's that record, isn't it?'

'Since you've guessed, there's no point in my denying it. Yes, that's what I'm after.'

'But how do you know it wasn't one of those crumpled ones which Miss Fox's murderer scattered about the floor after killing her?'

'I don't. But it mightn't be and it's my job to exhaust all the possibilities.'

Helen frowned. 'Were you able to play back any of those records you found at Chambers?'

Manton shook his head. 'No, they were too much damaged.'

'So if you fail to find what you want at the Henhams, you'll have to presume that it was one of those destroyed on the night of the murder.'

'Or that it is hidden elsewhere – or that he never recorded a note of that particular matter.'

185

'I see', she replied thoughtfully. 'Well, what exactly is it that you want me to do?'

Manton watched her closely and said:

'Before we come to that, Lady Riley, can you tell me how it is you seem to know so much about what I want to look for?'

'Isn't it obvious?'

'What's obvious?'

'That you want to search the Henhams' house for this record.'

'Yes, but what record?'

'The one which Christopher made and which you think may provide clues to his death.' She looked at him with wide innocent eyes. 'Well, isn't that it?'

'Yes.'

'It was certainly no secret amongst his friends that Christopher used to make a record of practically every breath he drew. And after he acquired that dictating machine, he became more note-ridden than ever.' She studied her small, shapely hands in her lap and continued, 'But, personally, I very much doubt whether you'll find what you want at the house.'

'And why not?'

'Because he always kept those things in Chambers. He had no machine at home on which to play them back and so there was no point in keeping them there. My guess is that if it hasn't already been destroyed it's still somewhere in Chambers.' She smiled deprecatingly. 'But it's not for me to tell you your business, Superintendent. Now, what is it I'm to do?'

'I'd like you to invite Mrs. Henham, and the two Mr. King-Selmans to your house tomorrow evening.'

'But supposing they won't come?'

'I'm sure you can persuade them. You can always say that it's to do with the murders and spin them some sort of story on that line.'

'Like Miss Fox summoning everyone to Chambers the evening she was killed?'

Manton nodded. 'Yes. Will you do it, Lady Riley?'

'All right, I don't mind doing that. And while they're here, you'll be doing some official burgling.'

'It could be called that, I suppose', he said, with a short laugh.

'What time am I to ask them?'

'Any time convenient to yourself.'

'Am I to let you know the position after speaking to Celia Henham?'

'I wondered if you could phone her now before we go.'

Helen shrugged her shoulders and walked across to the telephone. She dialled a number and bit viciously at her lip while she waited for an answer. Suddenly she braced herself.

'Hello, is that you, Celia? Helen here. How are you, my dear? . . . I'm afraid this is terribly short notice but I was wondering if you and Mr. King-Selman and Robin would come round tomorrow evening? . . . Yes, tomorrow. There are one or two matters of common interest to us all which I think we should discuss. . . . You can? I'm so glad. . . . About eight. . . . On second thoughts, my dear, come earlier and have a bite of dinner. Make it about seven. . . . You will? . . . See you then, my dear . . . Good night.'

She replaced the receiver and turned toward Manton.

'As you heard, they're coming.'

'Excellent', Manton said and meant it. 'Will Sir Gethin also be in tomorrow evening, Lady Riley?'

'So far as I know.'

'I hope he won't mind. . . .'

'He won't have to, will he? I needn't tell him that I'm acting under your instructions.'

'Well, we'll be off. I'm very much obliged to you for

your co-operation and I'll phone you tomorrow evening
as soon as we've finished at the Henhams. Should anything go wrong in the meantime, you can get me at the
Yard.'

'Hislop will show you out', Helen said, as the maid
silently appeared in the doorway.

As soon as she heard the front door close, Helen drew
the telephone toward her and dialled Celia's number
again.

CHAPTER EIGHTEEN

THE next twenty-four hours were for Manton redolent of the calm which proverbially precedes the storm. He felt very much as he imagined General Eisenhower must have done in the hours before the Normandy invasion was launched. A plan designed for success had been made with all due care and now there was nothing to do but await events.

The greater part of the day he spent examining once more every detail of the case which his investigation had unearthed and by the end his few remaining doubts had vanished. Everything had fallen into place; everything pointed in one direction – to a cold and calculating murderer who had killed once with the utmost premeditation and unhesitatingly a second time to prevent disclosure; a murderer who somehow must be caught off balance if the chances of proving the crimes were not to remain infinitely problematical.

Promptly at seven o'clock that evening, Celia and her two escorts stood on the Rileys' doorstep. The immutable Hislop led them upstairs to the drawing-room on the first floor where Helen, outwardly cool but inwardly tingling with excitement, greeted them.

'Celia, my dear, how nice to see you. Let me take you to my room to leave your coat. Perhaps the men won't mind helping themselves to sherry.' The perfect hostess, she bestowed glowing smiles on Marcus and Robin as she led Celia to the door.

Robin immediately walked across to the tray which held a decanter of sherry and four glasses. He poured out two and brought one across to Marcus who was standing uncertainly in the middle of the room and scowling hard.

'We might as well make the most of the judge's sherry', said Robin, taking a great gulp. 'Why do you suppose she's asked us here, father?'

'I don't know and I don't like it. I wish your mother had never accepted the invitation. If I'd been there at the time, I could have stopped her.'

'We should get a decent dinner and that's about all', Robin said with unusual candour. 'I only hope I don't have to sit next to the judge.'

'I doubt whether he'll be here.'

'Good show.'

'If you look, you'll see that there are only four sherry glasses put out.'

'Oh, so there are.' In a puzzled tone he went on, 'I wonder what it is she wants to discuss?'

'Whatever it is, it didn't require our all coming here to dinner tonight', Marcus replied severely. 'You must be very careful what you say. This might be some kind of a trap.'

'Trap?' echoed Robin in simulated alarm. 'A trap for whom?'

'Here they come', Marcus hissed melodramatically. 'Don't forget: guard your tongue.'

'I'm so sorry my husband has been called away', Helen said, addressing herself to Marcus. 'I particularly wanted him to be present, but it's possible he may be back by the time we start our little chat after dinner. He's had to go to some meeting or other at the Lord Chancellor's office.

So many people think a judge's working day finishes when he leaves court, but I can assure you that it seldom does.' She turned to Robin. 'Be a dear boy and fetch your mother and me a glass of sherry.'

A few minutes later they went downstairs to the dining-room where an excellent dinner was consumed in an atmosphere of Tchekovian gloom, though without any of that dramatist's unflagging conversation. Robin alone seemed to enjoy his food and seemed intent on drinking as much of the judge's claret as he could induce the austere Hislop to pour him. Marcus spoke scarcely a word throughout, but sat glowering like a Neanderthal man brooding over the cave shortage. Celia responded abstractedly to Helen's flow of cultivated chit-chat and was obviously ill at ease. Helen, for her part, appeared unperturbed and natural, though Celia noticed that this was only a veneer, for on one occasion she stopped short in the middle of a sentence and listened with strained intensity when the front-door bell suddenly rang.

The meal came to an end and after Hislop had put a decanter of port on the table, Helen and Celia left the two men.

'We're having coffee in Gethin's study,' Helen said as she was going out of the door, 'not upstairs in the drawing-room. Now don't be too long over your port.'

'Robin, you've had enough to drink', Marcus said sharply as he saw his son down a glass of port like a vodka toast and reach out again for the decanter.

'Need something to keep the spirits up in this house of doom', replied Robin with a tiny snigger which became fused with a belch.

'You're tight', said Marcus accusingly.

'Nonsense. I'm just right. Anyway one must be forti-fied to deal with the showdown ahead.'

191

'How do you mean, showdown?'

'Don't you remember you called it a trap? The only thing is, who is going to get catched? You, Mummy, Lady Riley, the absent judge or *me*?'

Marcus got up and strode round the table to his son. Shaking him roughly by the shoulder, he said:

'I advise you to have two quick cups of black coffee and then to keep your mouth shut tight. One word out of turn from you this evening and I'll – I'll deal with you.'

Robin blinked, got up and obediently followed his father out of the room.

'Now,' said Helen, as she put down her coffee cup, 'shall we talk business? Oh, you'd like some more coffee, Robin? I think there's just enough in the pot.' She sat back on the wall settee and surveyed her audience. 'Yesterday afternoon, the police paid me a visit and . . . What's the matter, Robin?' She turned her head to see what it was that was mesmerizing his gaze and then gave an involuntary gasp herself. 'Oh, Superintendent, I didn't know you'd arrived. I never heard you. . . .'

'So you knew he was coming, did you?' interposed Marcus in an unpleasant snarl. He half-rose from his chair. 'I thought it was all some sort of a trap.'

'It's the showdown', Robin said oafishly.

'Yes, it's the showdown, isn't it, Mr. King-Selman?' said Manton looking hard at Marcus who was now crouching forward in his chair as if preparing to spring. For a moment there was silence and then relaxing his muscles he sat back and said slowly:

'I've no idea what you mean, Superintendent.'

'No? Let's start with your last lie first, Mr. King-Selman, if for no other reason than it's your biggest.' Manton's piercing blue eyes were fixed on Marcus's face as he spoke. 'Why did you lie about Miss Fox being alive when you left Chambers to get your cigarettes?'

192

'I didn't lie. She was alive', said Marcus in a throaty whisper.

'She was dead: battered to death and you know it.'

'Why should I know it? And anyway you can't prove a thing you're saying.'

'I accept that she was alive when you arrived'' said Manton, as if Marcus hadn't spoken. 'But I can prove that she was dead when you left a few minutes later.'

Marcus's face had become like a mask as not only Manton but Celia and Helen watched him under arraignment. Robin's mouth hung open and his hands fiddled with his pipe.

'That's true, isn't it, Mr. King-Selman?' urged Manton. But Marcus made no answer and Manton went on, 'You arrived, found Miss Fox alone in Chambers and killed her. Then you hurried away, only to return after some of the others had got there and to pretend that it was your first arrival?'

'That's very clever of you, officer. A shade too clever perhaps. If what you've just said is true, you can doubtless explain why I should ever have admitted going there twice.'

Manton smiled bleakly. 'The very point I put to Sergeant Talper when he propounded the same theory.'

'And I hope he gave you a satisfactory answer to this piece of fiction.'

'He said that you admitted the earlier visit because you must be sure you'd been spotted or that it could be detected in some way, and that therefore there would be less than no sense in your lying about it.'

'Very ingenious.'

'I agree,' said Manton pleasantly, 'but it doesn't happen to be the truth, does it?'

193

'I don't follow', Marcus said warily.

'It's quite simple. Miss Fox was, as I've said, dead when you left Chambers – and for the very good reason that she was already dead when you arrived. You were the first to arrive on the scene after the murderer had departed.'

'Then it wasn't father?' Robin said in a tone of evident surprise.

'No, despite the fact that it was he who removed the potassium cyanide from your laboratory after Mr. Henham's death.' Marcus flushed, but said nothing and stared stonily at Manton. 'You knew that, didn't you – or at any rate strongly suspected it?' asked Manton. Robin nodded but avoided looking in his father's direction.

'Then who did murder Miss Fox?' asked Helen.

'The same person who murdered Mr. Henham.'

'Not Mr. King-Selman?'

'No, despite all his lies and efforts to confuse the issues which may yet lead him into the dock of a criminal court. His motives in doing so may have appeared adequate to himself but the law doesn't take a kindly view of those who try and protect murderers. So far as Miss Fox's death is concerned', Manton continued, 'what did happen was this. He arrived at Chambers very soon after the murderer's departure. So soon, in fact, that he heard the murderer's hastily retreating footsteps and it wasn't difficult for him to recognize them as a woman's. . . .'

'Don't listen to his nonsense', said Marcus hoarsely.

Manton rounded on him. 'Can you for one moment deny that every move you've made, every lie you've told has had but one object; to cover up for the murderer?' He switched his attention to Celia, who suddenly went very white. 'And nobody could have done more,

194

could they, Mrs. Henham? His determination to protect you was so great that he was – is now – even prepared to swear that he was the murderer. But you and I know quite well that he isn't, don't we, Mrs. Henham?'

The question fell softly on the still air and faded away into an aching silence which was abruptly splintered by the telephone ringing. Helen slowly turned and looked at it as if uncertain what to do. Then she put out a small bejewelled hand and lifted the receiver.

'Hello?'

'Is that Lady Riley?' The voice at the other end came through with metallic clarity.

'Yes; who is that?'

'It's the Commissioner of Police speaking, Lady Riley. Can you come along to New Scotland Yard immediately? Something very urgent has arisen.'

Manton, who had recognized the voice, watched and listened. It seemed to him that Celia, Marcus and Robin had all stopped breathing in the taut atmosphere which now encompassed them.

'I – er – I'm afraid I can't come now', Helen said nervously. 'You see, I've got guests here.'

'This matter is far more important than any guests, Lady Riley.'

Then suddenly a new voice broke into the conversation. It was that of Mr. Justice Riley and its effect on Helen was of fire touching a piece of silver paper.

'You must go at once, Helen, and I'll join you.' There was a pause and he added, 'I'm speaking from the bedroom extension.'

'You're not; you're at Scotland Yard too. It's a trick', she screeched.

'Like the one you played on me the night of Miss Fox's death', he said with icy emphasis and rang off.

195

She looked desperately around. Her mouth worked uncontrollably but no words came and she seemed unable to let go of the telephone receiver which had gone dead in her hand.

Manton stepped forward.

'Are you ready, Lady Riley? I have a car outside. I must formally caution you . . .'

CHAPTER NINETEEN

IT was getting on for midnight when the peace of the
Temple was once more invaded and a small group of
people assembled in Christopher Henham's room in
Chambers. Manton had been considerably surprised that
Celia had expressed the wish to join them, but he supposed that she was determined to see the affair through
to the end herself and not rely on any second-hand account
of events from her son or ex-husband.

Manton bent over the recording-machine while Marcus
watched him with deep suspicion.

'For the hundredth time of asking *why* did she murder
Henham – if she did?' he asked gratingly.

'Be patient for a few more seconds and you'll hear',
replied Manton, without looking up. 'Now', he said a
moment later and into the stillness of the room there came
the voice of Christopher Henham: a voice clearly recog-
nizable though severely neutralized by the impersonal
machine which now regurgitated it.

'Wednesday 29th April 5 —', it began.

'The day of his death', Manton mouthed at his audience.

The voice went on: 'I spoke to Helen again yesterday
evening, but she is still adamant and refuses to compro-
mise. I have again given her fair warning that if she will
admit to being in the car with me, so as to clear Celia,
I'll take all the blame for the accident and support the
untruth that she was the passenger; otherwise I shall go

197

into the witness-box at Celia's trial and tell the whole truth, namely that Helen was driving the car when the unfortunate man was knocked down and killed. All this I reiterated to her last night. She now has ten more days in which to make up her mind whether to accept my offer or face ruination. End of note.'

'And that is why Lady Riley murdered your husband, Mrs. Henham: it also explains why she had time to prepare things so carefully, your trial at the Old Bailey being her sole dead-line.'

Celia shuddered. The expression was unnecessarily macabre.

'But when did she slip him the poisoned pill?' Robin asked.

'She had opportunities galore for that. She was meeting Mr. Henham almost daily to discuss their fix. As you know she's a very clever sweet-maker and she knew there was potassium cyanide at the cottage, hence what simpler than to make a lethal gelatine capsule to resemble a Capstick's Cough Capsule. That done, all she had to do was remove an innocent capsule from a tube which she'd bought and replace it with the doctored one. On the evening before his death, Mr. Henham stopped on his way home with her to buy a fresh tube of capsules and she then did the swap. After all, it wasn't very difficult for her to get hold of the one he'd just bought on some pretext or other and then hand him back the other?'

'But how do you know this?' Marcus asked.

'Cast your mind back to that evening, Mr. King-Selman, and you'll remember that when Mr. Henham came in he asked Mrs. Henham to open the tube he'd just bought as he'd hurt his hand. She couldn't do it and passed it to you. It didn't occur to any of you why that particular tube should have been more difficult to open than most. The reason was, of course, because it had been opened by Lady Riley and later resealed by her and she made a more effective job of it than the manufacturers.'

'And this . . . this show at the Rileys' house tonight. Was that necessary?' Marcus asked in a faintly disdainful tone.

'Yes; because although I knew Lady Riley was the murderer, I hadn't much hope of proving it without subjecting her to some sort of shock treatment. Yesterday I visited Mrs. Henham and, chancing my arm, took her into my confidence. What few doubts I had evaporated when she let me search her husband's study and I there found in a locked drawer the record you've just heard. Incidentally it is only one of several he dictated on the same matter.

'The next thing was to get the judge's co-operation and that proved to be easier than I'd expected. The truth is, I believe he had already begun to suspect that his wife was a practised murderer, otherwise why should he have rushed down to the cottage last Wednesday evening and removed the tin of poison? Obviously because he wished to cut off her source of supply for fear she should get further homicidal ideas.' Manton gazed round the rapt expressions of his tiny audience and continued, 'This evening, the judge attended a very high-powered conference at which he became completely persuaded of his wife's guilt and agreed to assist us.'

'Yes, that telephone call. What was that all about?' asked Robin, puffing hard at his pipe.

'It's very simple', said Manton benignly. 'The judge was in the same room as the Commissioner but pretended to be butting in on the conversation from his bedroom extension. You see, Lady Riley murdered Maureen Fox as she was speaking on the phone to the judge and then took the receiver from her dying hand and spoke to her husband, pretending to be upstairs in her bedroom.'

'Was it Helen, then, who was responsible for Miss Fox summoning us all here?' Celia asked.

'Yes. I suspect she came here that evening with the object of sounding Maureen Fox generally about the lie of the land – after all she naturally wanted to find out what Maureen knew or didn't know about your husband's death – and very possibly she hoped she might also get an opportunity of making a quiet search of this room. In the course of conversation, Maureen must have referred to seeing your husband and yourself – as she believed it to be – in the car together on the night of the accident and Lady Riley then immediately realized how perilous was her position. So long as Maureen believed it was you in the car, Mrs. Henham, she attached no significance to the fact that it was "you" in the driving seat and your husband in the passenger seat. After all, it was your car, so what could be more natural.' He looked at the intent faces around him and went on, 'At some stage Maureen told Lady Riley that you were coming about eight-thirty to go through your husband's effects and it was then that she conceived the brilliant idea of summoning all the rest of you here on the pretext that she'd suddenly seen the light and would solve the crime in your presence. She infected Maureen with her enthusiasm and she, poor girl, not realizing she was helping to bedevil the circumstances surrounding her own impending death, made all those phone calls, finally ringing up the judge.'

'Diabolical', said Marcus.

Manton turned toward him. 'It was, of course, Lady Riley's footsteps you heard pattering away as you arrived. But because you were so unconvinced that it was not Mrs. Henham who had committed the murders, you drew yet another false conclusion and told your biggest and most serious lie.' Discomforted, Marcus stared unseeingly at the floor and Manton continued, 'After you'd found

Maureen dead and had departed, the judge arrived. He incautiously got some of her blood on his shoe before deciding that these were no circumstances for a High Court judge to be found in and similarly departed. Next arrived Mr. Robin King-Selman and the rest you all know. . . .'

'When did you first start suspecting Lady Riley, sir?' Talper asked as they were driving back to the Yard.

'After she'd told me that the only cause of Henham's erratic driving on the night of the accident was his injured thumb.'

'Why that?'

'Because Henham was over six feet tall and the driving seat of the car was in the most forward position, and if he'd been driving, one would have expected that to have been a major cause of the accident. Don't you remember that young constable's report about it when he inspected the car immediately after the accident? He's certainly not six feet and yet he cracked his knee on the steering-wheel and had his legs all bunched up.'

Talper nodded his head slowly.

'Yes, there was only one suspect who would normally have driven with the seat as close as that, namely Lady Riley, and once Mrs. Henham was out of the running, it became a virtual certainty. The trouble was it took so long to eliminate Mrs. Henham, thanks to her extraordinarily quixotic behaviour.'

There followed a silence which was finally broken by Talper. He said:

'I should think the Home Secretary, when the time comes, would reprieve Lady Riley on the compassionate grounds of having lived so long with a man like his lordship. Gosh, what a pot of venom he is!'

201

'A pity they can't both be hanged', replied Manton.

'Do you think Mrs. Henham and King-Selman will remarry?'

Manton shrugged his shoulders in obvious indifference to their fate and said sardonically, 'Despite judicial formulae, divorce isn't as absolute as murder.'

THE END

›› If you've enjoyed this book and would like to discover more great vintage crime and thriller titles, as well as the most exciting crime and thriller authors writing today, visit: ››

The Murder Room
Where Criminal Minds Meet

themurderroom.com

www.ingramcontent.com/pod-product-compliance
Ingram Content Group UK Ltd.
Pitfield, Milton Keynes, MK11 3LW, UK
UKHW040435280225
455666UK00003B/87